LIPSTICK & LIARS

TE SHERIDAN

Lipstick & Liars

by

TE Sheridan

Contemporary Romance Novella

Published by TE Sheridan

Edited by A. Marie

Cover Photo: Deposit Photos

Cover Design by Redbird Designs

ISBN#: 978-1-951637-09-5

Sometimes I feel the need to remind people to watch what they say in front of me.

That being said, all it takes is a word or two, and my mind is off and running. It's all fiction, no matter what word or two is spoken, and no matter who the speaker and listeners are.

CHAPTER 1

AVA

When you take your wedding ring off after wearing it for nineteen years, you're making a statement. It's interesting to see the way people react. Some do a double take, like they have to be sure they saw a bare ring finger when you were talking about the new program you're working on, and you were gesturing wildly because taking your ring off wasn't natural for you and you forgot you did it, and so you don't think anything about it or try to hide it. Some try to be sly about it. They double take. They sneak a peek at your hands again when you stop talking and you're reaching for your wine glass, and some turn to look at a colleague, and they try to be sly about this, too, but you see the curve of their eyebrow, and you know they're thinking *did you know*? *What's that about? Have you seen Logan? Is he wearing his ring?*

He's not. Logan took his ring off first, and I didn't even notice until we were packing for this trip to Dallas. We're in the same industry, so we travel together often.

Used to be fun, but honestly, it got old after ten or twelve years. Take a fun, whirlwind romance and throw in bills and money and kids and all the drama kids can add to life, and let's not forget exhaustion, and those trips stop being a luxurious get away and become one more thing on the calendar. Kind of like making love. Should be fun, adventurous, special. Instead, it gets stale, and you resent the time you give to your partner because you just want a little *me* time.

Then again, it's not like that for guys, is it? Sex is *me time* for men, especially when they can roll over and go to sleep when it's over.

Logan was folding his button-down shirts to pack in his suitcase. He's a stylish guy—always has been—and I stopped what I was doing to watch him. The shirt he was holding was new, gray and white checked. I looked from the shirt to what appeared to be a new gray sport coat tossed over the end of the bed. Logan continued to pack, oblivious to my interest. I had my hair dryer in hand; I had planned to ask him to stick it in his bag as mine was jammed full.

"Mia's counselor—" I stopped midsentence. I remember that. Watching him as he packed his stuff meticulously. Thinking that he had a better wardrobe than I did. He keeps his fingernails cut blunt and clean. His hands are big and strong. And for nineteen years, he's worn a white gold wedding band on his ring finger.

"What about Mia's counselor?" he asked without looking up at me.

My heart hurt.

Not figuratively. Not like flowery-poetic-love-story-heart hurt. It hurt like when your ob-gyn presses and squeezes your ovaries during a pelvic exam. Pain that's sharp and severe and then when he releases you, you feel a little crampy and uncomfortable.

When I still couldn't speak, Logan piled the gray and white shirt on a pale blue shirt—folded just as perfectly— in his suitcase and looked up at me. He wears glasses sometimes instead of contacts, and recently, he switched from the wire-rimmed rectangle lenses he's worn for years to fashion frames.

My husband of nineteen years was dressing like a twenty-year-old guy and not wearing his wedding ring.

Yes, before you ask, I'll just tell you. We're going through some things. At twenty-five, when we got married, I was naïve enough to believe we were different. We were wildly in love and crazy about each other, so there wouldn't be any bad times. Nineteen years later, I know better. Show me a marriage without strife, without growing pains and blow ups, and I'll call bullshit.

We talked about separation one night before we were packing for Dallas, but *we* hadn't made any decisions. Apparently, Logan did. Without telling me. Symptomatic of our marriage, I guess.

"Logan." I dropped the hair dryer on the bed and propped my hands on my hips.

"What?" He straightened, the scowl on his face almost more familiar to me now than his smile. "What'd she do—"

Mia, our seventeen-year-old daughter, has a long history of getting into trouble, so I could almost forgive his scowl. But I felt like his fingers—including his bare ring finger—were squeezing my neck and cutting off my air.

"Really?" I whispered. A flash of guilt eased his scowl to a slight frown, but Logan avoided my eyes. "Now?"

"We talked about this, Ava."

There was no anger in his words. Just regret. Defeat. I think that's what scared me most. If Logan was done with anger, done with shouting matches, we had already moved on through the second stage of marriage. I remember fear of losing him, of losing our life together, chasing a chill up my spine, over my skin.

He swung his gaze to me, his blue eyes pinning me in place. They used to turn me on; now they were cool and indifferent, and if there's anything worse than anger or even hatred, it's indifference.

"But we didn't—. Logan, we didn't decide…"

He hissed a sigh and propped his hands on his hips. The aggression in his stance made me move. I felt like a stranger, an unwelcome, *unwanted* stranger rather than his wife. Hunching my shoulders, I folded my arms over my chest to protect myself.

"I think it's for the best," he mumbled.

The best for whom?

I didn't ask. Truth? It might be. For a few days. For a short time. Mia and Jake used to moan and groan over our public displays of affection. Logan used to be the husband who couldn't walk by me without patting my ass or copping a feel. We used to hug a lot. Snuggle on the couch for evening TV. Close and lock the bedroom door even if the kids were up and running around.

These days we're either at each other's throats over bills or the kids or the dog, or we go days without acknowledging each other. Sure, Mia's behavior puts a lot of strain on our marriage, but I'm sure our issues are beginning to bleed into her behavior. Detention's become a regular thing for her, and I doubt Logan and I fighting all the time is good for Jake. No, marital problems don't cause learning disabilities, but I'm sure the stress, the tension in the house, makes our son feel anything but safe.

Breathing room could be dangerous, though. Which is why I didn't give in before when we talked about a trial separation. While the thought of not feeling judged on every move I made was appealing, making it real—living apart for just a week, even—felt like giving up. The beginning of the end.

Logan has a thing for Charlotte Benz. I've heard the whispers. Always a flurry of them whenever Logan and Charlotte are in the same room together. Funny, there's something about a whisper that's so much louder than casually spoken words. Maybe because they imply something bad, something that should be hidden. People tend to rubber neck a whisper just the same as they do fatal traffic accidents.

Logan's decision to take his ring off before we left for Dallas felt fatal.

Even if I wouldn't have heard the whispers, I knew. Did our colleagues, our friends, really believe I could sleep beside my husband every night and not know he was attracted to someone else?

We finished packing in the uncomfortable kind of quiet that makes you feel like you're bumping up against each other's space and the accidental touches are unwelcome, so you hurry to get done and end up more reckless, and it just keeps happening. Logan slept in the spare room. That alone might not have been so bad, but the way he said goodnight was painful and awkward.

He spoke to my reflection in the mirror in our bathroom. In his athletic shorts and the T-shirt that showed not only his hard shoulders and wide chest, but also the beginning of a spare tire around his middle, he met my gaze for a few seconds. I paused in the act of washing my face—the skin around my eyes itchy from the tears I hadn't been able to stop earlier when we were packing.

He started to say something, but he drew up short and just stopped and pressed his lips together. My throat too tight to talk, I waited. Logan hung his head for a second, and I had the ridiculous thought that maybe he had changed his mind and was going to say so. That rather than living apart and letting the problems in our marriage grow bigger to fill the space between us, we should work on them together and let our love fill in that space.

But he only huffed a quick breath and looked up at me again and shrugged. The way his voice broke when he said goodnight—just *goodnight,* not *goodnight, Ava,* not *I love you*—didn't mean much, because the shrug killed me. Another vicious squeeze on my heart.

I knew Charlotte Benz would be in Dallas. She got married a few years ago, and for a while, I was naïve enough to believe that made everything okay. I had watched them flirt, and I laughed it off with the rest of the gang, because I believed that Logan loved me.

I went to bed that night wondering if Logan loved me *enough.*

CHAPTER 2

LOGAN

Speculation does damage. So, maybe it wasn't the right thing to do, but at dinner that first night in Dallas, I just told everyone: the colleagues I was there with—some of them I consider close personal friends, and so does Ava—and some of our clients. We were having drinks before dinner. Max Russell ordered a bottle of wine, and Ruby Donaldson was having a draft beer, and I was sipping on Old Forester bourbon. Maybe someone at the table had noticed I wasn't wearing my wedding ring, but no one had mentioned it. I kept patting my pants pockets and then my stomach, and maybe it looked like I was checking to make sure I hadn't forgotten anything, like my phone. In reality, I was making sure I had clothes on, because I felt naked without my ring. After nineteen years on my finger, the sudden absence of it was heavy, and I saw myself dragging my left hand around like a cartoon caveman with a club.

I don't know who started the conversation, but we

were going around the table talking about how we met our spouses and when we started dating. Something nagged at my gut as Ruby shared her story about meeting Marty at an off-track betting parlor. Everyone teased her a little bit, but she explained that Marty was there with a group of friends for a twenty-first birthday. Ruby was interviewing for a cocktail waitress job.

I liked the topic, because it makes me feel good to think of how Ava and I met. I was crazy about her, and I would have pursued her to the ends of the earth to have her. But sharing how we met just dredged up the stuff Ava and I had been going through the past year, and I was uncomfortable thinking about telling them.

But somehow lying, trying to pretend things were okay, seemed worse.

For the first time ever, I had booked my own room, apart from Ava's. While I needed that space—for no other reason than needing to stretch out and sleep in the whole bed, to leave my worn clothes tossed over the end of the bed and not see Ava roll her eyes as she picked up after me—I wondered if I had sent the wrong message to my wife.

To our friends and colleagues.

I had my glass at my lips when everyone swung their gazes to me. I sipped the Old Forester and held it in my mouth for a second, not because that's what you do with whiskey, but because I needed one last second to pull myself together and just say what needed to be said.

"So." I swallowed and took a deep breath as I lowered the tumbler to the table. The place was packed, and I had to speak up a bit over the low rumble of conversation around us. Next to me, Garrett Shaffer was looking at something on his phone. Garrett and I came up through the ranks together at iTec Solutions, and he knows me almost as well as Ava does. He thought he could listen with one ear while I talked because he knows the story of me and Ava meeting well enough to tell it himself. "Ava and I are having some issues right now."

Garrett snapped his head around to look at me and made me think of that scene in *The Exorcist*. The hand holding the phone—the one with his wedding ring— dropped to the table, and he stared at me like I was speaking Greek. I saw a few others wince, maybe in understanding, maybe just in regret, and it made me feel better and worse both.

In for a penny, in for a pound. I kept going.

"You know. Just stuff." I shrugged, and my hand was still wrapped around the whiskey tumbler. I almost picked it up for another drink, but I wondered what that would say about me, so I didn't. I skated my eyes around the table, quick eye contact with each of them. "But..." I swallowed hard, and my skin itched where Garrett's stare was burning through me on my right side. I could have explained. I could have said that Mia got arrested last month for drinking and driving, and I could have told them that Jake wasn't making progress with his vision therapy or that Ava forgot to make the orthodontist payment, and she was angry with me for wanting another new big screen TV, but each of them probably had their own horror story they could have shared. And most likely, it would sound a lot like ours. The difference being that everyone has a different breaking point, and I was currently at mine. Relativity, also. Nothing can hurt you as much as your own sad story, your own loss, whether it's by divorce or death.

I didn't share more than that. I didn't give them our details, and I didn't tell them we were doing a trial separation. Instead, I dug into the past and told them that twenty years ago, I met Ava on the job. She was working at Bergmann when I started at iTec. I saw her at a meeting. She was cool and collected, this beautiful girl who looked like a model, but she was warm and easy to talk to. She had this great laugh; it invited you in and made you feel welcome, like you'd known her forever. I didn't tell her until we'd been dating six months that I had sold my soul to the devil to arrange our working together. Rich Akers put me in charge of the division that worked directly with Bergmann, and eventually, Ava skipped out on them and joined the iTec ranks.

She was smart, and I was as attracted to that as I was her sweet smile and perfect ass.

I didn't say those words that night at dinner, but I'm pretty sure that sometime in the past nineteen years, I've said as much to Garrett. He knows about the night Ava and I fucked in the storage room before our first official date. Ava doesn't know he knows about it, and Garrett and I don't revisit it, but there've been a lot of late-night rambling sessions over too damned much liquor for things like that to not slip out now and then.

Dinner went okay, but I felt the undercurrents of the things I said bouncing around the table. Garrett and Max did that silent communication thing at least ten times, as if I wouldn't notice. I wondered when the rumors would start, because once I'd said something, I decided it was a mistake. Garrett and Max were probably wondering about Charlotte Benz and what she had to do with the issues Ava and I were having.

There's nothing going on between me and Charlotte. We're good friends, but Charlotte and Ava are good friends, too. Granted, Charlotte and I used to flirt a lot. We pushed things past a limit, and there was that one night. Things got a little heated, but that had nothing to do with Ava, and none of it has anything to do with what's going on with Ava and me now.

On the flight that morning, I forgot for a minute that Ava thought I wanted to leave her, and I started talking to her about one of our clients. Seated next to me on the plane, I felt her body tense when I started talking, and when I quit, when I had posed my *what if* scenario to her and I was waiting for her thoughts, she finally turned her head to look at me.

Her sleepless night was mapped in the whites of her eyes, in the bruised skin around them. She had done her makeup, and though I could see how much I had hurt her the night before, she looked beautiful. She tended to gnaw on her lip when she was upset or overthinking something, and that morning, she had skipped her usual pink lipstick. On the flight, her lips looked dry, and I wanted to kiss her.

I didn't try, though. She saw my eyes lower to her lips, and she looked away without saying a word. I don't know what she was thinking. I feel like I never know what Ava's thinking anymore. We parted ways at hotel registration. I thought it would feel good to be on my own for a bit, but mostly, it felt like giving up, like failure.

We finished dinner, and I couldn't help but wonder what Ava was doing. She had dinner plans with other clients, and I found myself wondering what she ordered. If she was drinking wine or gin and tonic, and if she drank too much, who would walk her up to her room? Garrett ordered chocolate lava cake for dessert, and Barbara, the waitress, brought it out with seven forks, and everyone oohed and awed over the warm chocolate, and I squirmed in my seat, needing to move.

Ava and Mia don't get along well, and I know my wife is ready to lock the kid up and throw away the key. Mia is willful and strong, much like her mother, though neither of them see it that way. Mia doesn't think before she speaks or acts, and the end often justifies the means, and Ava has made several unplanned trips to the school to deal with disciplinary problems. I think—well, no, I *know* —Ava gets frustrated with that. She's embarrassed, for one thing, that Mia sometimes displays the mouth of a sailor and the manners of a feral child. It's more than that, though. Ava has begun to resent that she is the parent the school contacts about Mia's poor choices and bad behavior. Ava works fifty-hour weeks, the same as I do, and it's not fair to her that she is often dealing with Mia's punishments when she has work to do.

We walked back to the hotel after dinner, and everyone was complaining about how full they were and how they needed the walk to work off the calories they had just consumed. I was right there with them—miserably full and happy to walk—but I also craved some space and fresh air. Nineteen years with someone at your side is hard to walk away from, and with each step, I changed my mind on what it felt like.

Freedom. No one constantly nagging about finances and kids and the leak in the kitchen sink. No one asking for me to put gas in her car or check the noise the engine is making. No one disappointed in my performance, needing more, when all I want is to roll over and go to sleep.

I thought when Ava and I separated, it would be easier. I thought letting go of all of that might make me a better man. I would have more time to myself, more time to exercise which should make me sleep better, which in turn, would make me more productive at work and at home.

I didn't think about other women; I definitely wasn't thinking about Charlotte Benz when I tugged the band off my finger.

I didn't want to add another complication in my life. I wanted to make things simpler. Another woman would destroy Ava, and hurting Ava would hurt my kids, which was the last thing I wanted to do.

CHAPTER 3

Ava

Dallas was awkward. I was still reeling from Logan just making the decision to leave me—I'm not being dramatic, separation felt like the beginning of the end of our marriage. It hurt. Every damned thing a woman can wonder about dragged me down as I sat through workshops with our colleagues and meetings with clients. Was it because I had aged? The crows' feet around my eyes? The lines around my mouth? The weight I hadn't been able to lose after Jake was born? Had age changed my body enough that Logan wasn't interested anymore?

Or had he finally chosen Charlotte over me? Had they been together all this time and suddenly made a decision to go public? Was it someone else? Was he in love with someone else, or did he suddenly feel the need to play the field and hook up with random women? Younger women, more attractive and energetic and exciting?

Or was it just that the issues we had to deal with on a daily basis had become so big, we couldn't see each other through them or around them anymore? Maybe it was just that we had spent so much of the past year—or two, if we're being honest—parenting and being mundane, responsible adults, that we had forgotten who we used to be, and how we used to love each other.

And maybe Logan just didn't love me anymore.

It's hard to pretend everything's okay when your whole world feels threatened. Logan's announcement the night before we left for Dallas left me feeling panicked and unsteady. Mia and Jake didn't notice anything, but it was a rushed morning when we left, and anyway, the world revolves around you when you're a kid, so why would either of them have an inkling something was wrong?

Our friends, though. Our work friends. How do you hide that? Every time I took a breath, I had a stab of pain in my side, in my heart. There was a knife in my throat that made talking—just greeting other people—nearly impossible. Any outward concern made me feel worse. I had no intention of telling anyone anything. If anyone asked where my ring was—damned right I took mine off, because I refused to be the clueless, trusting wife when Logan was free in Dallas—I only shook my head to let them know it wasn't something I wanted to discuss.

In Dallas, no one asked. People noticed. Of course, they noticed. Neither of us was wearing our rings, we didn't check in together, didn't sleep in the same room, and probably spent three minutes talking from the moment we arrived until we checked out. Those three minutes were jammed with tidbits regarding Mia—an F on an Algebra test—and a client.

Not us.

Four weeks after Dallas, we went to Philadelphia. You might think that was easier, but it wasn't. If anything, it was worse. During those four weeks, Logan moved out. The kids were stunned to realize for just that moment that the world didn't always revolve around them, and both of them gaped at Logan like he was a stranger as he carried things to his SUV. I watched from the kitchen, until I couldn't watch any longer and turned my back.

After sleeping alone in Dallas and wondering if Logan was alone or enjoying someone else's company, we came home to the same damned things. The dishwasher had started leaking, and Mia rear-ended someone in the parking lot at school, and Logan slept in the spare room and then one day, he started boxing up a few things, and I watched him haphazardly toss pieces of our lives into that cardboard box and walked out of the room, afraid he would find pieces of me there to accidentally take with him.

I listened, though, with my back to him as he explained his leaving to the kids. Mia was hysterical, and by then, she had turned the whole thing back around to herself. How could Logan leave her? And Jake? He was their father, and he owed it to them to be around.

Words like *temporary* and *lease* and *trial separation* bit into me while he sweet talked the kids until they both came around. Never mind that my husband of nineteen years had just packed his college diploma and an old camera and a few framed photos from vacations past into a box and lugged it all out to the SUV to leave. Never mind that he hugged and kissed them both and didn't spare me a glance as he mumbled something about calling me as he left.

He called, but we talked only about the kids and the upcoming trip. I bristled at his suggestion that we just drive to the airport together, since we were living together at the time we made the flight plans. Logan must have sensed it; apparently, I'm often aggressively argumentative, so he started throwing out reasons to defend his suggestion before I could say a word. When he finally stopped talking for a moment, I told him to pick me up the morning of the flight, and then I hung up, and I sobbed my heart out.

I've read some articles now about marriages in crisis, and I'm seeing people say eventually you run out of tears. The pain might linger, but the tears will finally stop and leave you cried out and lost, and finally, numbness will set in. I'm not there yet. I'm still crying.

Logan didn't notice.

He had the nerve to smile at me the morning we left, as he pointed at a to-go coffee he had picked up for me. I fought off the overwhelming desire to dump it in his lap. I considered ignoring him and letting it sit there and get cold. But the petulant streak passed, and as angry as I was with him and as much as I hated him for putting the separation in motion, I loved him. I wanted him to see that, to remember me and come back. If I went with every crazy impulsive bad idea I had, I would probably drive him right into another woman's arms.

I wasn't sure I could forgive infidelity. Not like this. Not if he had purposely set me aside to stretch his legs and play around for a bit, thinking he deserved a break from his tedious marriage. Not if he thought he could have a free pass and come back when he was ready.

I drank the coffee, but I'd already had coffee before he

arrived. I wasn't eating. If he noticed I was losing weight, he didn't mention it. He had to have seen that I had the shakes as we printed our boarding passes and checked our bags. Since we travel so often, we're both TSA PRE check security, so we stood in awkward silence and waited for the short line to move along. Logan texted someone rather than risk looking around and making eye contact with me, but once we were through security, he took me by the hand and dragged me to the sports bar near our gate.

I let him lead me, but once there, I yanked my hand back from his and sat across a table from him, not next to him. Logan ordered a burger, and when I only asked for a small salad, he clucked his tongue at me and asked for a second burger, eyes on me as he spoke to the waitress.

I took my iPad from my carry-on, and rather than look at him or struggle not to, I went through emails and then when I had checked enough that I had a massive headache, I surfed the web and priced new dishwashers while Logan kept his eyes trained on the TV hanging in the corner of the bar.

I knew about Logan's grand announcement in Dallas. About how the day after he took his ring off, he felt it necessary to make a statement while he was having dinner with colleagues and clients. Remember, whispers tend to draw more attention than a regular conversation, so before that night was over, I knew what he had said and who he had said it to.

Philadelphia was harder because while the separation was still just beginning, we were four weeks in, and he hadn't changed his mind. Four weeks in, and our colleagues were lighting up the grapevine, and I wanted my old life back. Yeah, after seventeen solid years of good times, we were reeling, but I wanted to push through it. To tackle it and hold on and come out on the other side. The good times had been the best of my life, and knowing that Logan didn't value our life together the same as I did, crushed me.

Running into Charlotte in the lobby of the hotel in Philadelphia only added insult to injury. She hugged me, just the normal hello hug, and maybe I was just being overly sensitive, but she held on a little too long. Like she knew. Like she felt guilty. Which might simply mean she felt guilty because she knew there had been whispers that she and my husband had a fling a few years ago. Or that she felt guilty because she and my husband did have a fling a few years ago. And maybe decided to rekindle the flames.

Trying to decipher it made me angry. I was probably rude to her, and yes, I'm aware that if anyone was watching the exchange, causing a scene would only have given them more to talk about. No scenes, just me with the sort of stiff-arm hug and a frosty hello and slipping away from her as quickly as I could. You know, it hurts to lose a friend almost as much as it hurts to lose your husband. Charlotte and I used to be close enough to chat on the phone for hours or close a bar down and swap stories and secrets over mixed drinks.

Logan and I had separate rooms again, so once I was checked in and managed to escape Charlotte before she could hit me with questions, I went straight to the elevator. My mistake was looking back. Like a pinball, Charlotte bounced off me and straight into Logan's arms. I looked back just in time to see his lips brush her cheekbone.

Not remotely sexual, and something I've seen him do a hundred times. Some people kissed hello; some people kissed me hello.

But not Logan.

He hadn't touched me other than the bumping into me the night we packed for Dallas and earlier in the airport when he tugged me into the bar and ordered that extra burger for me. And no, I didn't eat it. I couldn't have, if I had tried.

I ducked into the elevator before either of them could see me watching them, but the damage was done. Maybe there was nothing between them; maybe there never had been. But when you're looking for things to justify how much you hurt inside, you'll find them. Even knowing Logan had good reasons to be frustrated with me, even though I started half the arguments and rarely backed down once I sank my teeth into something, I needed to find reasons to be angry. Otherwise, the hurt would swallow me whole.

Charlotte, though. She was reason to be angry, sure, but it hurt. The thought of my husband's arms around her in the lobby in front of everyone tore my heart out. Or maybe it was my lungs, because once I stepped into my room, I struggled to breathe. The heavy door closed too slowly, and so I gave it a hard shove and then fell back against it and slid to the floor to cry.

I had dinner plans, though. With clients. So, I had to pull myself together. Funny, the harder you try to get your shit together and be presentable, the more you fall apart and the uglier you are. I finally stripped off my clothes and took a scalding hot shower. I was chilled, and I was desperate to wash away anything Charlotte might have left on me when she hugged me.

Later, when I was walking with Madelyn Hendricks and Jason Smith, to Chip's—a wine bar for a drink before dinner—I felt someone watching me. You know that feeling when someone is watching you, and the hair on the back of your neck raises; I know you do. I turned, and of course, Logan and a different group were across the street heading who knows where for a fun night. He lingered at the corner for a moment, though, to stare at me.

I hesitated. I thought he would walk across the street. Not to go down on his knees and grovel. Not to ramble on about making a mistake. But just to see if I was okay. He used to hold my hand when we walked in big cities like this, and he used to hold me in his arms when I was upset about the kids or my parents or his mom, and he used to say just the perfect thing to make me smile.

He sized me up—no other word for it. Nothing like making a scene. His eyes roamed low over my silk navy tank—low cut, yes, but I was wearing a white leather jacket over it, as I had done many times before—my skinny jeans—yep, Logan, even wives who can't shed that last five to ten pounds of baby weight wear them—and the low-heeled black boots I had only purchased a few days ago.

The wind picked up and whipped my hair in front of my face. It was too damned cold out to stand and watch him and wish on stars. He tucked his hands in his hip pockets and rocked back on his heels. He wore jeans, too, and the purple button-down shirt I had bought for him at a Columbus Day sale before he decided to leave me.

"Ava!" Madelyn called as the light flashed that we should walk. "Let's go, woman! It's freezing out here!"

It was, but I think my nipples were hard from Logan's penetrating gaze, not the temperature. I missed him. He took a few steps backwards, eyes still locked with mine. I had the ridiculous thought that we should have made love the week before we went to Dallas. But we hadn't. It had been a rough week. Long hours at the office. Arguments with Mia about a college visit she had cancelled without our knowledge. Disappointment that Jake wasn't making enough progress in his vision therapy, and in seventh grade, was reading at a fifth-grade level.

The last time we had sex, Logan was just getting over a sinus infection, and he had tweaked his back shooting baskets with Jake. It was less than good, and now he was free to roam. Window shopping could now be hands on, shopping for texture and taste.

He turned finally, and the spell was broken.

"Ava!"

I captured the hair that the wind had blown into my lipstick and pulled it away. Madelyn reached for me as I stepped off the curb, and we huddled together to brave the wind as we crossed the street, heading in a different direction than Logan and his crew.

CHAPTER 4

Logan

The red lipstick.

Jesus.

In all the years we've been together, I've never seen Ava with bright red lips. She usually wears a sweet pink color, though in the winter, she tends to wear something a tiny bit darker.

We were walking, Garrett, Travis Harms, and me. After the drive to the airport and the morning in the bar and sitting by Ava on the plane—God, yes, I needed a beer. I needed testosterone and beer and football, and so, we were going to this bar to have a drink before meeting some others for dinner. Garrett was talking about a stripper he'd seen somewhere; apparently, her moves and her rack had left quite an impression on my friend.

I was laughing, because that's what you do, right? Mob mentality. Boys being boys. Whatever you wanna call it; Garrett was describing her tits, and I was trying to play along and not wonder what Garrett's wife, Tricia, would think about her husband spending most of his free time in strip clubs, and I heard her voice.

Ava's.

No, actually, I heard her laugh. Funny, because it's been a damned long time since I've heard her laugh. Probably longer since I've made her laugh. But there it was, on the corner outside the conference center hotel in Philadelphia: Ava's gushing, happy laughter.

Garrett didn't notice; I mean, no one's gonna know my wife's laugh better than I do, right?

I wanted to ignore it. I wanted to keep walking. I was desperate for that beer. Ava's silent treatment was killing me, and I was mad that she was treating me like everything wrong between us was my fault. I'm man enough to take my share of the blame, but it's not all me, and it only pisses me off more when she gets all righteous on me.

I couldn't, though. I couldn't just keep walking. I had to peek. How in the hell could she be laughing when our lives were in this upheaval right now? She was with Madelyn Hendricks and Jason Smith. Madelyn's okay, but Smith is a douche. He's always got his hands on a woman. Any woman who crosses his path. And tonight, my wife was in his path.

The thought of him sitting by her for drinks, leaning in close and putting an arm around her to share a snide comment, or pressing his thigh into hers as he leaned around to say something to someone else made me see red. Ava isn't crazy about him, either, and yet, she was standing with him and Madelyn, and while I watched, she tipped her chin up and dropped her head back for a full throttle laugh.

The thought made me think of her when we're in bed together. The soft little purrs in her throat when we're making love and the way those purrs rev up to full-volume moans of pleasure, the way she tips her head back and exposes her neck to me. Yeah, standing on a street corner in Philadelphia with thoughts of fucking my wife in my head and a full-blown hard-on in my jeans.

She caught me staring. I should have turned away then, because as she turned to look at me, I remembered the fight we had a few weeks ago, right before I decided I needed a break. Jake hadn't latched the gate in the back-yard, and the dog got out. Charlie's a German Shepherd, and apparently, he scared a kid a block over and bared his teeth at him. The woman who called and complained about it to Ava went so far as to accuse Charlie of biting the kid, but I don't think the dog would bite anything. He's big, and he looks fierce, but he's a lover.

Ava hadn't wanted a dog in the first place, as she kindly reminded me after the phone call. I get it. No one likes an ass-chewing, and if it's undeserved, it's that much worse. The kids and I had ganged up on her with the dog, and even though we finally softened her up on that, she had come unglued when we brought Charlie home. She assumed we were looking at small dogs.

That fight—the one that started out about Charlie and turned into every damned thing I've ever done wrong in our marriage, and after nineteen years, it adds up—was a blowout. We were in our bedroom, and the door was closed, but the anger picked up steam for both of us, and before long, we were screaming at each other, and not only did the kids hear every word. I'm sure the neighbors did, too.

The tank top and leather jacket were sexy as fuck, and again, red-blooded rage rolled over me at the thought of Jason Smith looking down her top or copping a feel. The painted-on denim accentuated her sexy hips, and I remember thinking about digging my fingers into her skin to grip her hips when we fuck against the wall.

It was the red lipstick, though.

That red lipstick and the tug of memory, the thought of her lips wrapped around my dick that stole my breath away. Madelyn started hollering at Ava; the light had changed so they could cross. And then Garrett must have realized I had fallen behind, because he was yelling at me, giving me shit about keeping up and that middle age was pretty hard on some men. I remember thinking it wasn't so much middle age, but maybe, middle marriage. The beginning is great; the honeymoon phase when you're so over the moon for your wife, and either you're always snuggling up together or you're boning anywhere you can, and maybe—hopefully—if you make it to old age, you retire together and travel and experience the world on a laid-back mature level, but maybe the middle sucked for every couple.

"Oh, shit," Garrett mumbled as he moved up behind me. "C'mon, man. Let 'er go."

I wanted to punch him just then, and like I said before, Garrett's a close friend. But you don't stick your nose in and dick around with your buddy's marriage, ya know? Who the hell did he think he was to tell me to let Ava go, as if we were already completely over, and I should be happy to move on?

"C'mon, Logan." Garret nudged my arm with his elbow. "She's with Madelyn. She'll be fine."

That comment mollified me. He wasn't suggesting that my marriage, that Ava, wasn't worth the fight. Just that tonight wasn't the time to tackle the problems. Who knows? Maybe he was even acknowledging that the douche was with my wife, but so was Madelyn, and Madelyn would have Ava's back.

I wondered, though, when I turned and Garrett and I caught up with Travis again, if that meant Ava was going to party tonight. Would she? Would I? I didn't in Dallas. Was this any different? In some ways, it felt different, but mostly, it didn't.

The biggest difference was that I had moved out of the house. Nothing official. My driver's license still had the same address that Ava's did. My mail was still delivered to the house Ava and the kids were living in. But, yeah, I had packed up the important things—some clothes and my toothbrush and shaver—and leased a small loft apartment downtown. Ava watched me the night I was throwing stuff in my bag and in a cardboard box, as if I couldn't be trusted and if she turned her back, I might throw her mother's silver in so I could hawk it for spending money.

Apparently, I wasn't supposed to take any framed photos, because she got pretty pissed at me for the few I tossed in the box. I mean, I don't know how long I'll live there, and yeah, I need some space. That's the whole fucking point of needing to have my own place for a bit. But I still needed my kids in that space. I still needed Ava; I just needed her at a distance.

Garrett bought the first round, and I sipped my drink slowly, barely listening to his and Travis' conversation. The bar was already pretty packed, but then again, it was a Saturday night. You learn to expect no less.

If Ava and I split up, I would end up with the dog. Unless she decided to keep him just to dick with me. Yeah, Charlie could be a pain, just like having another young child. He was a big responsibility, but I loved the damned dog. What if Ava decided to keep him because she knew it would hurt me? We hadn't always operated on choosing what would hurt each other the most, but it happens in marriage. Don't pretend you don't get what I mean. Sometimes, you hurt so much about something so small that your wife has no idea what the problem is, and the only thing you want to do then is lash out and hurt her back.

Misery loves company, blah blah blah.

I was still stewing over Ava and the kids when we left the bar and walked to a seafood restaurant to meet the rest of the group. I had shoved it all to the back burner, but it was still there, simmering, and I wasn't in the mood for the chatter about NFL standings. I like football, but I'm not a die-hard fan; but some of the other guys are.

I didn't get drunk. In fact, I switched my hard liquor for a light beer. Drank a couple of glasses of water and ate a big steak. I was fine when we left the place, but I hunched my shoulders and tucked my hands in my pockets as we walked to another bar for after-dinner drinks, and I wondered why I wasn't cutting loose and getting drunk. I didn't have to indulge to the point that the guys would have to roll me out the door, but why not tie one on just for fun?

Because it wasn't fun. Because even though I needed the space from Ava, I had been joined at the hip with her for so long, I didn't know how to operate in that space without her.

We ended up in a bar where people were jammed butt to nut, three or four deep. No tables to be had, but a bunch of us crowded near the far wall—at the end of the bar—and stood and talked. Garrett and Travis were still around, but I found myself caught up in an industry conversation with Alan Mefford and Liza North. Work stuff was easier to do without Ava, and eventually, I realized I had relaxed, and I was back to drinking the hard stuff. Shoulder propped on the wall, I sipped my drink and listened to Alan's concerns on his company losing federal funding. I scanned the room behind him over his shoulder. I think most people do that. Maybe it's just a natural instinct, to make sure everything is as it should be. Or maybe it's simply that you look around now and then to break any intense eye contact that might be happening. Whatever the case, I was looking around when I saw Charlotte near the opposite end of the bar.

Ava is a brunette. She's worn her hair in all different styles and lengths. Not gonna pretend to know what the hell I'm talking about when it comes to women's styles. But Ava is pretty, sometimes sexy, sometimes sporty and cute. She's always been every good thing a man wants in his wife. Even when we wake up together on a weekend after a hard night of partying and short night of sleep, I've always found Ava attractive.

She's been wearing her hair short and sleek. It's sexy as fuck, even though I was a little bit crushed when she cut it off last time. She's short, which she claims makes her look even dumpier. Granted, there's more to the woman I married now than there was twenty years ago, but the curves are soft and feminine, and I love to put my hands and mouth on them, so you're not going to hear me complaining.

Charlotte is pretty much the polar opposite of my wife. Tall and willowy thin. Long, flowy strawberry blonde hair. While she doesn't have a lot of the curves Ava does, I've had her body pressed up against mine a time or two, and I'm pretty sure I'd love to put my hands and mouth on her if I wasn't married.

She's with mutual friends, of course, and her cheeks are rosy red. Probably from the cold air outside, but also probably from alcohol. I don't know where she puts it, but she drinks as much or more than I do and never seems to gain a pound.

I watched Charlotte for a few moments, but because I knew everyone was watching me those days, probably just waiting for me to fuck up just one too many times and have Ava banish me forever, I didn't stare. I tuned back into the conversation with Alan and Liza just in time for Garrett to wander back over to us.

"What the fuck's goin' on with you, man?" He elbowed into the conversation and kind of hedged me back away from Alan and Liza. He spoke quietly, so most likely, neither of them heard him, but it still rubbed me the wrong way.

"Me?"

"Well, rumor has it you moved out." Garrett shrugged. Guy rules say you don't maintain a lot of eye contact when you're having a serious talk like he was attempting, so his eyes roamed the bar rather than watching me. "Why're you leaving Ava, man?"

"I'm not leaving her," I grumbled. Garrett swung his gaze back to me. He lifted his drink to sip from it, eyes on me now, eyebrows crawling up his forehead. "Right." He nodded, but he had the sense to look away.

"Lotta stuff goin' on." I should have left it alone, but I couldn't. Once again, I had moved out temporarily because I needed space, and that just automatically made me the bad guy.

"Yeah? Well, Tricia's dad was just diagnosed with cancer," Garrett announced. "And Harper broke her arm last night at a sleepover at her friend's house. And Tricia and I got into it about the car."

"What about the car?"

"What?" Garrett shot me a frown. "The car's fine, but she wants something new. That's not even the point."

"I know what your point is." I downed the last of my drink.

"You still got it for Charlotte? Is that it?"

"No." I spoke firmly, because I wanted no question in anyone's mind that this was about anyone but me and Ava. "There's nothing with Charlotte, man. Ava and I can't occupy the same space for five minutes without wanting to kill each other."

"Tricia threw a shoe at me last Monday."

I shrugged and laughed when I saw the ghost of a grin on Garrett's face.

"You probably deserved it."

"Yeah, F.Y.I. Don't ask your wife for a lap dance immediately after returning from a business trip."

"Dumbass."

Garrett shrugged. "Ironically, the trip was quick and quiet, and there wasn't much happening in the way of fun stuff."

"I don't know how we're gonna work this out."

Garrett shot me a frown and then he kind of winced, like my words caused him pain.

"You love her?"

"Yeah." I nodded. "Just not sure it's enough anymore."

CHAPTER 5

A<small>VA</small>

If you asked him about Jason Smith, Logan would say he's a tool. He's okay. He's easy on the eyes, and that night in Philadelphia, easy on the eyes worked for me. Jason's fun; he's old enough to know better, but he's a flirt. Kind of the same as Logan's friend, Garrett. The difference is that Garrett is Logan's friend, and I think Logan would follow him if he jumped off the bridge. Jason's divorced, so it's not like his flirting hurts anyone.

Logan's once-over out on the corner left me feeling unsteady again, and over drinks with Madelyn and Jason, I was stewing over the fact that not only did he leave me, but he still had his hooks in me and still had the power to hurt me. Everything about loving Logan hurt, but maybe believing that he didn't love me anymore hurt the most.

Madelyn and Jason spent the time over drinks talking about colleagues and what was going on in their lives and life in general. It struck me while I listened to them bat around the possibility that Joy Coben might be pregnant again—noteworthy because she has seven kids and she just turned forty—that somewhere, other colleagues were betting on the odds of Logan and I staying married. Mostly, that kind of talk isn't vicious, though I know at times it is. I'm as guilty of it as the rest of the world, but that night in Philadelphia was an eye opener.

What were they saying? Most likely the entire group there at the conference knew that Logan and I were having problems—thanks to his tucking his wedding band away and announcing that we were dealing with some things. And though I hadn't told anyone that Logan had moved out, I'm sure he told Garrett, and so yeah, I'm sure the whole industry was buzzing with that little kernel of knowledge.

I wanted to know who put odds on us getting through it and who had us divorced by the end of the next calendar year.

Over dinner, as we had clients with us, conversation steered more toward actual business, which was a relief to me. Not that I had much to contribute. It wasn't so much that I was constantly going over every argument Logan and I'd had through the years, although yes, I did find myself doing that a lot. And it wasn't that I was hung up on wondering what Logan was doing while I was with Jason and Madelyn, if he was with Charlotte.

Okay, that's a lie.

Years ago, when those whispers started about Charlotte and Logan, it got me. Add in the fact that Mia's reign of terror started around that time and that we were just learning of Jake's learning disabilities. We, and by we I mean I, spent most of my spare time at the school, either talking Mia out of trouble—though I quickly learned not to do that. My daughter is completely incapable of following rules and needs to learn one way or another that there are consequences—or working with Jake's teachers on his IEP.

My spare time was that three minute window when I might have my emails and laundry caught up, maybe I'd fixed dinner and had the kitchen relatively clean, and had to plan for a presentation I would be giving in two days, rather than the next day, and so somehow, it was always me dealing with the extras.

There were days I was so exhausted I would forget to eat, or I would go through the motions of a shower and then later realize I forgot to wash my hair. Logan helped. I can't lie and say he didn't, but it was never enough. If he threw in a load of towels or helped me change the sheets, he seemed to think he had earned a medal and a week of vacation. For me, that stuff never ended.

At the end of those days, sex was the last damned thing I wanted to think about. Some nights, I gave in, and we had average to mediocre sex. And sometimes, I pretended to be asleep when he came to bed. Either way, I hated it, and I know he did, too. Maybe Logan and I weren't the steamy stuff of movie sex, but we used to tear each other's clothes off to get a piece, like the first time we had sex in the storage room at the office. After hours, but there's always a slim chance of getting caught, and that added a little thrill to what we were doing.

It hurt to be so exhausted that I didn't want to be with him, but at that point, maybe it didn't hurt enough. Also, it's hard to be sexy, to feel sexy, when you look into your husband's eyes when you're making love and see the glaze of boredom. To lie beside him in the silence when it's over and wonder if he's thinking about someone else.

Somewhere between then and that night before we left for Dallas when Logan decided to take his ring off, the worry over Charlotte faded. Maybe because the whispers had quieted and maybe because Charlotte got married, and I decided that would make her less likely to be interested in my husband, as if somehow married women were less likely to cheat than married men.

In Philadelphia, I wondered about her, about them again. But mostly, I didn't contribute a lot to the business conversation going on around me because I was drained. My marriage was in danger, and the foundation of my life, of my kids' world, was crumbling, and somehow wireless networks didn't seem all that important to me.

We walked to another bar after dinner. There was a big group this time, and Madelyn was two steps in front of me, talking to mutual friends. I could easily have begged off and slipped back to the hotel room, but on the other hand, as tired as I was, I knew that once there, I would lay awake and worry.

I had no plans to pick anyone up and cheat on Logan. But damned if I was going to spend the night wallowing, alone, if there was any chance Logan was somewhere quiet, finally fucking Charlotte. The hell of it was, I had no way to know for sure what he did. If they were seen together that night, likely, the grapevine would have them sneaking off to her hotel room to spend the night together. And if I asked him point blank if he had been with her, he might say no.

And I wouldn't believe him.

As Jason and I brought up the rear of our little bar

hopping group, I wondered about wives who don't travel with their husbands. That aren't in the same industry. I know several couples who are, whether it's the medical field or education or communications like me and Logan —ironic, right?—but I wonder about Adrienne Phillips. She's an insurance agent back home; her daughter is in Jake's class. Adrienne's husband is an engineer and travels regularly overseas. Does she wonder if he's faithful? Or does she trust him explicitly?

If she does, is he deserving? Or is she naïve?

Or, what if Adrienne had a lover she snuck in and out all the times Doug was away on business?

I used to believe in the sanctity of marriage, but that night in Philadelphia, I realized I had my doubts. Not just about everyone, but most definitely about my husband.

Where were we, what were we, without trust?

"Penny for your thoughts." Jason draped his arm around my shoulders as we walked. The November temperatures weren't unbearable, but I had been cold since Dallas and wasn't sure I would ever warm up. I hoped that this was a friendship thing—Jason asking after me—and not a ploy to flirt with or mess around with the cliché middle-aged woman facing devastating changes in her life.

As the night wore on, I hoped I was tougher than the cliché middle-aged woman facing devastating changes in her life. Jason was friendly, not really any more so than usual, but to a woman in my position, it seemed so. You would think flattery and flirting wouldn't have a place in a strong, thriving marriage, but maybe that's the better place for it. Sure, when you make vows to someone in front of family and friends, those vows are a wall around your heart and your body and your spouse. But maybe in strong marriages, there are windows through which you're allowed to say fun, sexy things and not suffer consequences.

When your marriage is faltering and your faith in your spouse is at its lowest and you're not sure he loves you and if he does, maybe not enough to get through the tough times, flattery and flirting are a bomb, ticking and ready to detonate.

Madelyn hung close at the bar, and she and I swapped stories about our kids. Everyone knows Mia is a hellion, but most of our friends don't know the extent to which our daughter goes to start trouble. Madelyn does. She has three kids, and her oldest is a little bit like Mia. Although he's a boy, and he's twenty-two, and technically, an adult and so maybe the responsibility factor is different. Then again, her son is a heavy drinker, and rather than smarting off in class and pissing the biology teacher off, he could have a crazy night and get in his car and kill someone.

Twenty-two or not, I think I'd feel a bit responsible for that.

Jason stayed close, too, though and he threw out tidbits about his kids, about his ex. His kids were younger, seven and five. The five-year-old still sucked her thumb, and the seven-year-old liked to say the word *fuck*. But so far, they seemed okay with he and Lora splitting up. Jason still speaks of Lora kindly, though it's more like she's only an acquaintance and not the woman he created babies with.

I wondered how Logan thought of me, how he referred to me these days. How that might change if we ended up divorced. How in the hell had we gone from fighting about the damned dog getting out, which really was about Jake and his lack of responsibility and my babying him—Mia had overheard that and latched onto that fun, little nugget and relayed to any teacher and counselor listening that Jake was my favorite child—and the unnecessary spending and the forgotten bills and having the TV on too loud and too often and never having clean socks to me wondering if we would end up divorced?

"You never shared your thoughts." Jason nudged my arm with his elbow. My arms propped on the small, round cocktail table, he leaned further in and pressed against me elbow to shoulder.

"You never gave me a penny."

"I bought you a drink," he reminded me. "That's worth all the thoughts."

I sputtered a laugh as I reached for the drink. "That's so pathetic, Jason. My thoughts aren't worth the penny, let alone a thirteen-dollar mixed drink."

"It'll get better" he told me, and without delving into any of it, without acknowledging that anything needed to get better, I only shook my head. It wouldn't, and I feared that even if it did, it would have to get really ugly and much worse first. "I've been there."

"And where you are now?" I tipped my head at him. "That's better?"

"For me. For Lora." He nodded. "But I meant that you guys will figure this out."

It's surreal to sit in a bar hundreds of miles from home with a blue-eyed, dirty-blond guy who owns the scruffy look and has a smoking-hot ass, and always seems to know what to say to make a woman feel appreciated, and wonder just what the rest of the world knows about your personal life. So, Logan announced in Dallas that we were having problems.

Did he say more? Did he share over dinner what those issues were? Or did he wait until later and tell Garrett? I love Garrett, but I don't always love Garrett, and the thought of Logan telling anyone, even Garrett, all the secrets—good and bad—between us makes me feel physically ill.

"Yeah." I nodded at Jason and looked away because I just didn't want to get into any of it with anyone, least of all a guy. A good-looking guy. When a woman feels vulnerable and ugly, she needs a friend to build her back up, not teasing and cajoling. I didn't want Jason to fuel my worries over what Logan might be doing with Charlotte. I didn't want any laughing and teasing, and boys will be boys bullshit, as if even if Logan was fucking Charlotte or anyone else at the moment, it didn't count because he didn't mean anything by it, and there were no feelings involved. I didn't want to know if Jason thought my irritation with dealing with the kids and school issues was unfounded.

"How's Mia?"

Instantly on alert, I looked back at Jason, ready to jump down his throat for dragging my daughter into this. Whatever Logan had shared about our family was no one's business, and I planned to shut it down.

Apparently, I wore that aggressive mama bear mask when I looked at him, because he flinched and shook his head slightly.

"The last time we talked, she was having migraines," he reminded me. "In Dallas."

Chagrined, I sucked in a quick breath and mumbled an apology. I had forgotten that little detail. When we were in Dallas, I did mention something about Mia's migraines. I was talking to Jason and Madelyn. When Mia was younger, she was prone to earaches and ear infections, and I remember now saying in Dallas that she seemed to have traded in the ear issues for behavioral problems and migraine headaches.

"I'm not the enemy." Still pressed to me, elbow to shoulder, he leaned harder for a second, until I looked at him.

"I know."

"Do you?"

"It's hard." It was a coward's answer, and of course, this was hard. Stupid of me to fall back on such a trite phrase.

"Hard for everyone when this happens."

For a second, I wanted to jump on that and ask what *this* was, but I caught myself. For one thing, most likely, he was only referring to our separation. And if I made a scene about what *this* might be, the grapevine would be on fire before midnight. Again, not because people are vicious, but because people are people, and we all talk.

"Maybe worse when you're out haunting the same places together."

I expected him to agree just to change the subject. What guy wants to sit around and hash out feelings, especially bad feelings and especially when they aren't his own? Unless that guy has ideas of scoring later, in exchange for being a good listener, and Jason Smith sure as hell wasn't so hard up, he was feeding me alcohol and a shoulder in exchange for sex in the back of the bar.

"Mmm." He nodded. "Maybe. Yeah. I get it. You're here. He's…"

I couldn't help it. My eyebrows shot up much too quickly for me to pretend nonchalance. Did Jason know where Logan was? What he was doing?

"He's out. Drinking somewhere else. With someone else." His eyes took a slow ride over my face, but I'm pretty sure they didn't dip lower than my lips. Pretty sure only really hard up guys are the ones checking out my boobs nowadays. It crossed my mind that if Logan and I divorce, and I ever crawl out of my cave and manage to stand on my own, I should get a boob job. Fake boobs don't droop.

And then it hit me that I'd had too much to drink if I could frame a possible divorce as a way to improve my looks and my sex appeal. Who cared? Fixing my boobs and getting some fat sucked off my hips wouldn't do anything for who I am inside, and that's who Logan is falling out of love with.

I don't love getting older and feeling unattractive, but it makes my heart hurt to think Logan doesn't love me anymore.

"You probably wonder if he's talking about it." Jason quirked an eyebrow at me, and I jerk my mind back to the current conversation. "I don't think he is, Ava."

"I should go," I mumbled, probably not for the first time.

"It's hard, though. When you're apart, too. Lora decided she was single enough when I was gone that she was okay with being single. She learned not to need me."

What he said made me think of what I was thinking of before, wondering about Adrienne and Doug. And other couples separated often for work. Not just fidelity and trust issues. Independence ranked right up there, I supposed. Part of me wanted to rally for Lora; why should she hang around and wait for Jason to remember she was there? But I snuck a peek at Jason, and honestly, he looked miserable, and I didn't know their story. How could I sit there and worry over what people were saying about me and Logan and then turn around and judge someone else?

"Yeah." I nodded and sipped my drink. "I suppose it is."

"I'll walk you back to the hotel," he announced when I put my empty glass back on the table. A moment ago, that statement would have dragged me back through the wondering about sex and cheating and left me feeling more insecure about who I am. But after that little peek at Jason with his guard down, I figured he was just concerned about my safety.

"It's okay." I shook my head. "I'll be fine, Jason."

"Not gonna let you walk several blocks alone here at night," he argued.

"I can get a cab."

"I can walk you." He shook his head and slid off the bar stool. I teetered a bit on my feet when I stood, and I remembered the days when I wore sexy heels, and Logan always wanted me to leave them on when we were fucking. When had that stopped? When had everything sexy and fun between us stopped and morphed into middle age? When had we stopped being Ava and Logan and become the McKinleys? Married forever, parents of two pain-in-the-ass kids we suddenly loved more than we loved each other, occasional lovers but mostly more like companions?

My bladder was ready to burst after three or four rounds of drinks, so I excused myself and slipped back to the ladies' room. I wasn't drunk, but on any other night, I might have said pleasantly tipsy. There wasn't much pleasant about that night, though. I stood for a moment in the restroom, waiting to take my turn, and I was privy to a conversation between two girls about whether or not to do a sex tape with someone named Pain. When they emerged from their stalls, I was stunned that neither looked much older than Mia. Possibly college students. Because the mom in me desperately wanted to tell them no on the sex tape, and I already felt like I was a million years old, I ducked into the nearest stall without a word.

I peed a river, and I read the graffiti on the walls. Somewhere between seeing that Alli was a slut and Colin had a big cock, the girls walked out of the bathroom, and I was left listening to some techno mix of a pop song I hadn't liked in the original version. It hit me as I was zipping my jeans maybe the girls should do the sex tape. Yeah, the Internet was scary as hell, and once something like that was out there, it was out there. But what if they reached my age and looked back and realized they'd lived a pretty boring, toe-the-line life and regretted the chances they didn't take?

Why didn't I run track in high school? Should have. Why didn't I punch Barbie Jenson in the face sophomore year when I saw her hanging on my boyfriend? Why did I tell Bobby Iverson no in college when he wanted me to come to his dorm? Bobby wasn't the star quarterback. He wasn't a stellar student. In fact, he dropped out the following year. He smoked pot, and he drank whisky, and he wore his hair long. But he was sexy as hell, and I heard through that good old grapevine that he had an incredible tongue and was particularly skilled at oral sex.

I was afraid.

Things with Logan used to be good. Maybe not off the charts crazy like that. We'd never recorded ourselves having sex. We'd never invited a third into our marriage bed. We watched porn together, but only once in a while. We'd walked through adult toy stores together and laughed at the whips and chains, but we'd never done anything unconventional.

At the sink to wash my hands, I sized myself up in the small, dirty mirror. I was older now. Had some lines around my eyes and bags under my eyes, some recent courtesy of Logan. I had a few spots of gray in my hair, but I colored it religiously. My hands had some age spots, but I kept my nails meticulous and pretty. My boobs had never been centerfold quality, and after two pregnancies, they looked a little worse for the wear.

But I had loved Logan with my whole heart and soul, and I had given him the best years of my life. Now it was me feeling inadequate and broken when he was the one to give up and walk out.

Jason was waiting for me at our table. Eyes on his phone, he started moving with me as I walked by him. I hadn't taken the time to freshen my lipstick, even though all traces of the new bright red were gone now. No need to primp and give anyone the wrong idea. I had simply hit the wall, and I was ready for bed.

"So. Garrett and Travis and Logan are down the street," Jason told me as we stepped out into the night.

"Logan and I have different rooms." I folded my arms over my chest as we walked, cold again in the wind. "He moved out a few weeks ago."

Jason cringed and stuffed his hands in his hips pockets as we walked. The expression was so heartfelt I knew he was surprised, and I wondered if I should have said anything. I pushed the worry out of my head. First of all, I had no doubt Garrett knew the second Logan's ass hit the driver's seat the day he left. Second, I was tired of shoving my thoughts, my feelings aside. I hadn't done anything wrong.

Everything bad, everything wrong between me and Logan took two to break.

"I'm sorry, Ava." Jason's voice was gruff. When I looked at him, he was staring out across the street, a deep frown on his face. "I hope you guys work it out."

"Thanks." I nodded and swallowed hard at the knife in my throat. "Me, too."

The streets were busy; weekend nightlife happening around us, but I was desperate then to escape it. Exhaustion hit me, and walking was a struggle. Maybe Jason noticed. He threw his arm around my shoulders again, but this time, he remained quiet.

The hotel lobby wasn't packed as it was earlier, but people spilled out of the bar there. It was possible my husband was in that bar. Maybe with Charlotte, maybe not. I didn't stop to look around, instead going straight to the elevator. Jason followed me.

"Thank you," I told him as I pushed the button. My left hand still looked foreign to me without my wedding ring, and I wondered how much longer it would be before it circled around, and I felt funny if I put it back on.

"You're welcome." He nodded, but when the elevator doors opened, he stepped into the car with me. Four people followed us, none of them familiar to me. Three floor numbers besides mine lit up, but Jason didn't touch the buttons.

I sank back against the mirrored wall wondering what the hell I was doing. Shame on Logan for entertaining thoughts of fucking Charlotte Benz, but here I was allowing Jason Smith to walk me up to my room. It was wrong, and honestly, I had no idea what was going through his head. For all I knew, his room was also on the eleventh floor, and the butterflies in my belly were uninformed and jumping the gun.

But I couldn't deny that I was curious.

Interested.

Tempted.

In one part of my mind, I knew I would be furious with Logan for just this much. For just standing near Charlotte and eyeing her breasts and her ass and wanting to maybe just touch her once. But in the other part of my mind, I was unzipping Jason's jeans and spreading them open.

He followed me off the elevator on my floor. Our eyes met as the doors closed behind us. The hallway with the gold and maroon carpet stretched out both ways from where we stood.

"I'm that way." He nodded to the left, and I felt something inside me break loose. Relief, yes, but disappointment, too. My room was to the right. Jason had been a gentleman to walk me back to the hotel, and though I had a brief moment of insanity, we were going to part company and say goodnight.

"Okay." I tipped my head to the right.

When I took a step that way, he followed me. I didn't question him. I didn't argue. I had no idea what floor Logan was on. I didn't know what I was doing. I didn't know how to be sexy anymore, and I wasn't sure if I wanted to.

My stomach clenched at the thought of what could go on behind a locked hotel door, but my throat hurt at the prospect of taking this step. So far, Logan and I were fighting over things out of our control. The kids. School. The future. Finances. The dog. Never mind that he'd had eyes for someone else once upon a time.

From the moment we stopped at my hotel door, whatever happened next was on me.

"You gonna be okay?" Jason's tight, low voice sent chills up my spine when I stopped at my door. My key card was tucked in my back pocket. I left it there when I looked up at him.

"Yeah."

Our eyes locked, we stood for a moment in the loudest damned silence I've ever heard in my life. My heart pounded so hard in my chest, if he had touched me there, he would've felt it. Instead, he reached for my hands.

When our fingers linked, it hit me that to me, this was cheating. If Logan and Charlotte ever stood hand in hand in front of a hotel room door and looked at each other this way, they had cheated.

"I don't know what's going through your head right now." He rubbed his thumb over the back of my hand. "But I've got a pretty good idea."

At that, my face colored, and I ducked my chin to laugh softly.

"I've got a reputation for this," he admitted. "Maybe I've earned it. You don't. I'm not gonna do something stupid to hurt you."

It was a pretty incredible thing to say to a married woman who was tinkering with the idea of infidelity. A pretty incredible thing for a guy friend to say to a girl friend who was going through bad stuff in her marriage.

A pretty incredibly worded rejection.

That's how my heart, my brain, my body, took it.

"I get it." I nodded, but I nodded too fast, and my voice broke, and I gave myself away, and then suddenly, I was in Jason's arms, pressed hard against him. For comfort. Not physical pleasure.

"You don't," he argued. "You look smokin' hot tonight, Ava McKinley. Good enough to eat. And if you were anyone other than my friend Ava and my friend Logan's wife, I would be on my knees begging you to let me come in."

I was glad to be tucked against him, my head pressed to his chest. My tears were hot and shameful, and my knees were weak, and my fingers curled around his shirt over his shoulder blades.

"I need someone to beg," I whispered, and then mortified to have said it, I held on tighter when he tried to look at me.

"I've been looking at you all night," he murmured over my hair. "I want what's in that skimpy little tank top, and I want those lips all over me, Ava. But more than that, I don't want you to hate me when it's over."

I nodded again.

I wanted everything. I wanted his hands and his mouth all over me, telling me I was still attractive, still sexy. But I knew he was right; I would hate him and myself if we crossed the line.

By telling me no, he was telling me I was loveable.

"I know." I finally stepped away from him and swiped at my eyes and laughed again when he tipped my chin up.

Down the corridor, the elevator hummed, and the doors opened, and we heard voices. We stood, eyes locked, and listened to those voices fade away.

"I would like to say he doesn't deserve you. I would love to spend the rest of the night pleasuring you." He stroked his thumb over my lips and then slipped it inside them when I gasped. "But I can't. Logan's a good guy, and nineteen years of marriage is a lot to give up for me, Ava."

I dropped my head back and thudded it gently on the door. Jason stroked the inside of my lower lip with his thumb, and then he dragged his fingers down my exposed neck, stopping at the lowest part of the V in the tank top. Technically, he was touching my breasts, and my nipples thrilled at his nearness.

Maybe he noticed. After all, I wasn't wearing a bra. With his eyes still on mine, he cupped my right breast through my tank and flicked my nipple with his thumb.

We had agreed not to do this, but his touch lit a streak of flame down to my clit, and I moved before I knew what I was doing. My hands were on his shoulders, and my breasts pressed firmly to his chest, and I kissed him.

Jason's mouth was hot and wet, and it was a soft, tender kiss, even with the flames inside me burning me up. Our tongues danced and slid together over and over, and I wanted his hands on my skin. It's easy, I wanted to tell him. I have nothing on under the tank.

I didn't say it, though. And his hands didn't wander.

His cock was rock hard between us, and I knew another minute would lead to more heartache and regret. Jason had been good to me tonight, and as desperate as I was for validation, for sex, I wasn't going to use him anymore than he would use me.

"Goodnight." I broke the kiss and then brushed another high on his cheekbone. He stepped away from me, chin down, and nodded. As he walked away, I saw him adjust himself, and then before I could do something foolish, I grabbed for my key and let myself into my room.

CHAPTER 6

Logan

I opted for the salmon this time, so I didn't feel as miserably stuffed the way I did in Dallas. The way I do a lot of the time. Sometimes I worry about heart disease and all of that health stuff that doctors are ramming down our throats these days. Cholesterol and erectile disfunction and mesotheliomia almost seem to be the new buzz words, and while now and then it hits me that I'm not young anymore, I don't live in fear of dying, either.

Garrett announced a probable merger between two key companies in our industry when we had finished eating. Travis gaped at him like he was thinking *no way*, but I mean, Garrett worked directly with one of the companies involved, so he would know, right? So then, Travis ordered up the next round, and Garrett kept talking about this merger. I was only half listening, though, and I felt like an ass. If the merger happened as planned, Garrett would lose the client. They were planning to swing their business to a direct competitor.

No shit, that would sting. Garrett's good at his job, and to just lose an account like that for no real good reason sucks. It wouldn't hurt him, really, in his position. He wasn't going to be in danger of losing his job over it, but no one wants to lose an account, and most definitely not because of a merger throwing business back the other way. Travis took it from there and launched into a story about the manager of Haslem Technologies being investigated for embezzling money.

That's bad stuff. I heard rumblings about that at the beginning of the month, but I hadn't dared to mention it. Apparently, the board of directors started doing some checking on the guy who suddenly had the money to buy himself and his wife new cars and build a new house. If the board sets your salary and you start living way above your means, an investigation is probably not out of the question.

I stayed focused enough to throw out a comment now and then, but I wasn't paying much attention. We had wandered down a few blocks after dinner and found another bar, and before we ordered our second round, Charlotte and Natalie Hoyer came in with some of their employees.

I watched Charlotte, but I tried not to be obvious about it. For one thing, I didn't want to draw her attention. And another, I didn't want Garrett questioning me again.

Ava and I had an active sex life, even if we didn't always burn up the sheets. I never went to sleep without what I needed, but there were nights now and then when I couldn't seal the deal for her. The fact that no matter how it played out didn't affect my sleep bothered her. Now and then we talked about it, and now and then we experimented, and sometimes, Ava had to do it herself. I used to get hard watching Ava get herself off. I love watching her, but that buzz word—ED—I don't know, it loomed in the back of my mind. I'm in my mid-forties, and I don't usually have a problem with it, but I'm not as hard as I used to be. While I love fucking my wife, I also love a good night's sleep. I've never meant that to hurt Ava; it's just what age and complacency do to a guy.

Maybe to a marriage.

We haven't had sex since I left. Before that actually. And I know she wasn't satisfied the last time it did happen.

I sipped my scotch and watched the room. Big city weekend night life played out before my eyes. Music pumped around me, that damned techno beat that makes young kids think twerking is the only kind of dancing. I'm a guy; sure, I love watching women shake their asses and grind on someone. And married or not, I'd love to be the guy on the dance floor with pretty girls in skimpy skirts and big tits grinding on me.

But as I drank that night, the music and Garrett and Travis talking around me, I watched the girls and wondered if my daughter danced like that. Granted, Four Heights wasn't a big city by anyone's standards, and there was only one club there, and it was a relic from the 60s. But Mia went to parties. High school parties were wild back in my day; I shuddered to think of what they were now. Ava hadn't been that crazy when we were younger. So, okay, I met her after college, but if she wasn't wild then, I can't picture her as being a crazy student. But she knew how to drink, and she liked sex, and suddenly, my chest was tight, and I couldn't breathe.

Where was Mia right that instant? What if she was the girl to dance like that? To take her clothes off for someone?

Suddenly, Charlotte was standing in front of me. She waved her fingers in my face and gave me a careful smile when she realized she had my attention. I probably looked like an ax murderer sitting there wondering about Mia. Did Ava know these things? They didn't get along well on the best of days, but I wanted to think that Mia confided in Ava about girl stuff.

"Hey." Charlotte eased in to stand by our tall table. Natalie Hoyer had moved around to the other side. Arms looped around Garrett's neck, she leaned in far enough to hug him that all three of us could see her breasts and the black silk that was supposed to hide them.

"Hi." I flashed Charlotte a smile, but I didn't feel like being friendly. Nothing that had ever happened, none of the stuff between me and Ava was her fault, but I was beginning to feel cramped at the table. My knees were stiff, and I couldn't catch a full breath.

If Ava moved just right tonight, her breasts would be on display just like Natalie's. What was that about? She always looked beautiful, but she wasn't usually one to show too much skin. I didn't like it, and now, I wished I had taken the time back there on the corner to tell her that. She had no business slinking around with business associates dressed that way.

"What're you drinking?" Charlotte leaned in to put her lips at my ear. The touch of them there, the feel of her breath on my skin, and the vibration of her voice at my ear reminded me of other things we had done. My dick gave an unwelcome twitch.

"Dewars," I answered.

"Need another?"

I sighed and looked around again. The same girls were still grinding their asses into the same guys' dicks. The same music was still blaring. Natalie was still hanging on Garrett, and while I honestly didn't believe he would ever do anything to hurt Tricia, I wondered suddenly where Garrett drew the line. Ava told me once years ago that she didn't trust him. We had gone to dinner with him and a few other colleagues, and when we were back at the hotel, she flat out told me she thought Garrett would fuck anyone that moved.

I eyed him for a second now and wondered. He had his arm around Natalie. His eyes kept dipping to take in her perfect tits. Natalie's young, and she's not married. No kids. She's bubbly and fun, and I'm guessing incredibly fuckable. I imagined unbuttoning her blouse and finding her tits encased in black silk. Finding a black silk thong between her legs. Bending her over and taking her hard, not having to worry about making her come. Girls like Natalie are all about pleasing men. They don't need anything in return.

"Logan." Charlotte nudged me again. When I pulled my eyes away from Natalie, Charlotte's grin told me she knew exactly what had me so distracted.

"No."

I could have had another drink, but I was done with the atmosphere. The music was giving me a splitting headache. The skin on display making me so fucking horny, my zipper was in danger of my dick busting through it. Enough bullshit. I'd had enough. For years, I had been playing this game. The fast-paced industry was exciting and fun, and there was potential for continued success. But I was tired of the constant travel and the hits it was taking on me and my wife.

"No?" Charlotte sounded surprised.

"No." I stood up. "I'm headin' back," I told Garrett. Arm around Natalie, still—I could see his hand wrapped around her waist—he nodded at me, glanced at Charlotte, and then back at me with a cautious frown.

"Night." Garret nodded. Travis and I exchanged a few words, and then I was ducking out, heading for the main entrance. Charlotte tugged on my hand to get my attention.

"Wait for me?" she asked. She arched an eyebrow and nodded her head back toward the interior of the bar. I figured she had to use the restroom, so I nodded and stepped just outside to wait. When the door closed, the music faded, and big city night was my new soundtrack. The sounds of cars, the engines and incessant honking. A blip of rap music as someone crept up to stop at a light.

Garrett read the situation wrong. He had to assume I was leaving to be with Charlotte.

It wasn't a bad idea. Charlotte and I had shared a steamy kiss and a heavy make out session a few years ago. Nothing we had planned. I don't know what it is about her. I mean, she's gorgeous, but so is Ava. She's funny, genuine, giving.

So is Ava.

Maybe it's just that she's not Ava. And after eleven years of marriage, I was curious about what was still out there. If I still had any appeal, any game. It had happened in New York; Ava was at home in Four Heights. Mia had fallen and broken her arm in three places the day we were supposed to fly out. So, Ava stayed with her. I checked in with them several times all weekend, but in the early morning hours on the weekend, Charlotte and I ended up in my hotel room.

Ava called as I was sliding my hands under Charlotte's skirt. My fingers were on her thighs, her skin hot on mine. Her breasts—smaller than Ava's but firm and gorgeous—pressed against my chest. We had kissed so much, her lipstick was gone, and her fingers were on the button of my jeans when my phone rang.

It was after midnight, so I assumed it was an emergency when I saw Ava's name on the screen. Charlotte had dressed quickly and slipped out as I tugged my undershirt back on and dropped to sit on the bed and answer the call.

Ava caught that I sounded out of breath, and I lied and said it was because the hour and the buzz of the phone scared me. She promised me everything was fine, but she missed me, and she hinted around that she wanted phone sex. My cock was like steel, but I was still thinking of Charlotte's heat under my fingers, so I told Ava I couldn't. That I was with Garrett in a bar.

We talked for a few minutes, and then she said she loved me. I mumbled it back to her, and I know now that she's thought about that night a hundred times or more since then, and I haven't really given it thought since, except that night in Philadelphia.

Charlotte emerged from the bar and curled her arm around my back and leaned in as we walked.

"Does she know?" she asked without preamble, and I

wondered if there were really guys who fessed up even if they weren't under the gun.

"No."

"You never told her?"

"No."

She nodded.

"Sometimes I hate her for that phone call."

Her confession made me angry, because even though Ava only suspected as much and even though there were only whispers and no proof, I've seen the way that night hurt my wife. I can't take it back now, and even though the separation has nothing at all to do with Charlotte Benz or any other woman on the fucking planet, Ava and everyone else in my life seemed to believe otherwise.

"And sometimes, I'm so thankful she interrupted us."

I looked down at her as we walked and recognized the sincerity on her face.

"I wanted you that night, Logan," she continued in a soft, breathy voice. "I still do. But I don't wanna be that woman. I don't wanna be a homewrecker."

"Everyone we know thinks we're fucking right now."

"I know." She nodded. "And there's a part of me that thinks why not? If they think it anyway, shouldn't we have a little fun with it?"

My dick did a full throttle rev, and I dragged my eyes away from her. Yes, I still wanted to strip her clothes off and lick her from head to toe and fuck her fifteen ways from Sunday. But not the way I wanted Ava.

Ava and I have fun. Besides the obvious. Even when it's hot and heavy and wet and hard, there's something to laugh about. With Ava, I want to make it as good for her as for me. I want her to come unglued under me. I love the feeling of her pussy clenched tight around me, convulsing with her orgasm.

And when it's done, and we're panting like we've sprinted for miles, and we're sweaty and I throw my leg over hers, she doesn't shove me away. In fact, she rolls over to get closer to me. One of us always ends up laying in the wet spot, but we just hold each other and touch each other.

It's because I love her, and I've never loved another woman. And even though I still believe Charlotte is sexy as fuck, I'm not interested in something that will drive my wife further away.

"I can't, Charlotte."

"I know." She nodded. She sounded a little bit sad but mostly okay. "I don't wanna hurt Ross."

I felt a little niggle of relief. There went my man card. The fact that Charlotte was so close to me, that she's so friendly and giving, sometimes makes me feel bad for her husband. It makes me wonder if all women, all wives, have that same tendency to cheat. If they watch the same frenzy of skin and sex on a dance floor and instead of seeing smooth thighs and perky tits, do they see hard shoulders and nice asses and hope for big packages?

Would Ava cheat?

Had she ever had a moment with someone the way I did with Charlotte?

Funny that I could rationalize the things I did with Charlotte and keep it separate from Ava. The fact that I find Ava sexy and Charlotte sexy, and that I can appreciate both women for their differences, and that I almost had my cock inside Charlotte and say it was just that we were away from home, and I just needed that break. Just needed to find my game. Hit some pussy and feel good about myself again. Forget the nagging wife and the kids and the upkeep of homeownership and bills—

What if Ava needed all of that, too? What then? Would I let it go and forgive it?

Why make vows if you were that willing to cross your fingers for a time out any time temptation struck?

"Wanna get a drink?" Charlotte looked up at me when we stepped inside the conference hotel. The hotel bar was dark and quiet. I saw people mingling, but from where we stood, they appeared to be our age and dressed in real clothing, not clothes made for dolls.

"Sure." I followed her into the bar. Charlotte went after a tall cocktail table in the corner and I went to the bar to order. Another scotch neat for me and a glass of pinot for her. I refused to feel guilty for knowing what to order her; we've worked together for far too long to not know. I waved to a couple guys from Memphis as I carried our drinks back to our table. Frank Lohman runs Regency, and Aiden Miller is a marketing guy from Spotlight.

Charlotte and I weren't doing anything wrong, but again, I felt their eyes, their suspicion, on me as I sat down across the table from her.

"So." She sipped her wine and eyed me with mean green eyes. "What the fuck, Logan? You went from having a few issues to moving out on her?"

I wonder if Ava has told anyone that. I did tell Garrett, and yes, I knew when I told him that even though he and I are the best of friends, it would eventually get out. Then again, I was living in a loft apartment small enough to fit inside the main floor of my home, and I was living there alone, and my late-night entertainment featured TV. I wasn't entertaining other women.

"I needed some room," I mumbled, and for the first time, it hit me how stupid it sounded. Either Ava and I were going to make it work, or we weren't. There was no trying; there was only moving. It was up to us to decide if we would move forward or backward.

"From what?" Charlotte shrugged. "What the fuck does that even mean?"

Ava says fuck when she's really pissed off about something or when she's really hot and revved up and talking dirty. I like a woman who can sit down and take a load off and cuss like a man now and then. It makes Charlotte one of the guys, and conversely, it's also something that has always turned me on about her.

"Logan!" Charlotte snapped.

Maybe sometimes Ava was one of the guys. Maybe she threw words like fuck and cunt around like they were no different than the sight words you learn to read in kindergarten. Maybe her sailor's mouth turned other guys on. I know damned good and well that tank top she wore that night turned Jason Smith on.

"She hates the dog."

"Good reason to leave her," Charlotte agreed sarcastically.

It wasn't my reason; it was the straw that broke the camel's back, and it was a place to start. I ignored Charlotte's jab and kept going.

"She didn't want a dog to begin with."

"So, this is just me." Charlotte drummed her nails— short and clear—on the tabletop and shrugged. "I'd probably keep Ross and get rid of the dog. Just sayin'."

Her sarcasm grated on my nerves and made my head pound.

Where was Ava? What was she doing right now? I scrubbed my hands over my head and took a deep breath.

"So, Jake and Charlie were in the backyard, and Jake took Charlie out for a walk. Or something. I don't even know what the fuck happened, but Jake left the gate open and Charlie got out."

Charlotte, eyes glued to me now, only nodded.

"So, later, we get a call. Ava answers it. It's a woman a block over complaining that Charlie scared her kid. That he bit her."

"Uh-huh." Charlotte tipped her head and waited for me to say more. "It's still easy to fix. You get rid of the damned dog, not your wife."

"It spiraled."

"Really?"

"Enough with the fucking sarcasm, Char," I groaned. "This is my marriage you're using for stand up."

"Bullshit. You did this, Logan."

"She babies Jake."

"He's what? Twelve? That old? It's okay to baby your kid. You know what, Logan? I can't. I can't baby any babies, because I can't have any. What the fuck is wrong with letting her baby her son?"

"The kid's gotta grow up some time," I told her.

"Did you have to get rid of the dog? Put him down?"

"No. Because Charlie doesn't bite. The kid could have tried to pull his tail off, and he wouldn't bite."

"So, you let this fight blow up into Jake needs to learn responsibilities, and Ava cleans up his messes?"

"It's not just that, Char."

"Then what is it? You moved out, Logan. You packed your bags and moved out. That's as good as telling Ava she's not worth the time. Your marriage isn't worth saving."

"I never said that."

"Have you guys talked about anything? Are you seeing a counselor?"

"No."

Charlotte started to say something, but she apparently thought better of it. Instead, she sat back and crossed her arms over chest, drawing my attention.

"Was there ever anyone else? Other than me? The thing that happened between us?"

"What?" I whipped my head around to make sure no one was near enough to hear us.

Charlotte raised her eyebrows but said nothing.

"No."

"So, you and I almost had a fling, and then you get through, what? Eight more years of marriage? And you lie by omission to your wife about it. Which is fine, because I know it would kill her, and the last thing I would want to do is hurt Ava. But you get through that and leave her *now?*"

"I didn't leave. It's a temporary situation."

"That can't be resolved until you take the first step."

"It's so much more," I mumbled.

"Ross hurt his back at work. So, he's on prescription pain pills. I know he's hurting, Logan, but the drugs are killing me. They're changing him. He's lazy now. Tired. Can't focus. It happened six months ago, and he's still popping the pills."

I swallowed hard and looked away. Charlotte was

reminding me that sometimes life sucks for everyone, and you suck it up and move on.

"Mia was arrested for underage drinking—"

"I'm not gonna play one up, Logan. My life sucks right now, too, but I love Ross, and God help me, we'll get through this."

Rather than look at her, I chose to be a coward and picked up my drink. Scanned the bar for more familiar faces. Hell, maybe I was looking for Ava.

"I thought you wanted to fuck me." So much for behaving. I threw the words out with a snarl, because misery loves company, right?

"I do." She nodded. "Surprised, Logan McKinley? That married women who love their husbands still kind of wanna fuck around now and then?"

My stomach turned at the thought, and I saw red, but I couldn't take a swing at Charlotte.

"Like, I love him. I really do. He's fun, and he's interesting. Smart. We were planning a trip to the Grand Canyon next summer, and now I'm wondering if he's developing an addiction. So, okay, I'm looking at you, and I'm thinking of that night in your room and the way you kissed me. Like I was sexy. Desirable. You were so fucking hard for me that night, you could have drilled through a stone wall with your cock, Logan. Remember that?"

I did, and God help me, the dirty words coming from her mouth were enough to pump my dick up all over again. Even though I wanted Ava.

"Okay, well, now I'm remembering the last time Ross and I made love. The last time we tried. He couldn't."

Her eyes were glassy, which freaked me the fuck out,

because I don't do tears. It's bad enough when Ava gives in and cries. I didn't know how to handle Charlotte.

"I'm fine." She shook her head and dabbed at her eyes. "But he couldn't. So, instead, he did other things. For me."

How do you listen to a female colleague tell you over drinks that her husband performed oral sex on her? Why can I listen to Garrett talk about eating Tricia in the backseat of their car when the kids were little, and they had to sneak out to the garage to fuck around, but feel embarrassed when Charlotte tells me about her husband doing the same for her? Double standards, I decided.

"He was…" Charlotte cleared her throat. "It just wasn't good. And then, we had a blow out two days later, because I had a flat tire, and I didn't even realize it. Until I was home from work. I know what a fucking flat tire feels like, Logan, and I didn't notice it. I ruined the rim, and Ross went ballistic on me. And yeah, then there's that whole thing about me having to tell my husband that I can't give him children. Right? I mean, I know I'm not young anymore, but when we got married, we wanted babies. Never had an inkling there would be a problem, until there was a problem."

"Char."

"So, we have all of that going on these days," she continued. "And every time I go out of town and I'm free of that version of myself, the things that get to me are the most personal. They're me thinking what if he's feeling better but it's easier to be high than deal with me? Than face the fact that his wife is less than a real woman? I look at you and remember how bad you wanted to fuck me, and Logan, you're a good guy. I mean it. I love you. But you're not all that, and me wanting to fuck you now? It's because I see the way you look at me."

"Jesus."

Charlotte nodded. "I want to be wanted."

"This your long-ass round-about way of telling me how Ava feels these days?" I shot for sarcasm. I came close. Because even though her eyes were still glassy, she smiled and laughed softly.

"Just sayin' that as much as I love you, there's nothing special about you and what you're going through." She shrugged and pushed her glass at me. She had barely touched it.

"Charlotte." I said her name as she eased off the bar stool.

"Hmm?"

"Thank you."

"I might be wrong," she mumbled. "Don't thank me."

I watched her hips sway as she moved away from me. Called out to her again. This time, she turned to look at me but said nothing.

"The baby thing?" I said quietly. "Is he upset about it?"

She puffed up her cheeks for a second and stared at me silently. Finally, she shrugged and nodded and took a step backward. I wanted to console her, but too much had already been said, and there wasn't enough I could say to make her feel better.

"I'm not ready to go home, Char." I thought she was gone, but when I looked up from my drink, she was standing close to me again.

"Just be careful how long you stay away." She patted my arm. "Ava doesn't have to sit around and wait for you to reconcile. She's handling her end of this shit fine."

CHAPTER 7

AVA

Somewhere near forty—forty has been the worst *F* word I've ever used—my body started doing its own thing. The aforementioned boobs started to sag. The padding on my hips that came from Halloween candy and probably too much alcohol. The mysterious pounds that didn't add up, even after taking the Halloween candy and alcohol into account. The need for cheaters whenever I tried to read a nutrition label in a grocery store. The long nights of staring at the ceiling, when I should have been sleeping.

Sometimes, of all the fucking fantastic forty issues, I think insomnia is the worst. Because it not only keeps you wide awake and makes you feel like hell the next day, it provides you with hours of quiet in which you have nothing to do but fret over the rest of it. And then, because you worried about forgetting to pick up something for dinner the next night, or the ninth grader who rides your kid's school bus and bullies your kid, or the spot you found in your breast that's probably nothing but what if it's not, for hours, rather than sleeping like a baby like your husband did, you look even worse than you feel.

If I were naïve, maybe I would have thought that when Logan left, at least I would sleep. The snoring was gone, but I found that sleeping alone in a bed for two was uncomfortable. After nineteen years of curling into him, of feeling his heat, the safety of his body next to mine, I decided I could learn to live with the snoring again if he ever came home.

Hotels are loud, and the one in Philadelphia was no different. I was awake at one when a loud, most likely drunk, group passed by my door. I was irritated, but why? They didn't wake me. No, I was irrationally angry and jealous that someone was out and having a good time when I had retreated to my room to wallow in self-pity. Okay, really, I was angry with Logan for making me feel so small and alone. By leaving me, by taking his ring off, he had left me feeling alone to deal with the kids and the household responsibilities, and by announcing it to our world, our friends, he made me feel othered, when we were with colleagues. Like I should be wearing a red letter on my chest. Not an A for adulterer but maybe N for not quite good enough or a U for unlovable.

I loved him.

And I hated him.

Kissing Jason had left me with a ball of sexual need and only my hands to take care of it. I wish I could say I didn't, that I was above it. But it had been weeks since Logan touched me, and that tiny little stroke of Jason's thumb over my nipple was my undoing. Touching myself took the edge off, but I was lying awake and thinking some about Jason. What it would have been like if I had invited him into my room. I wondered what kind of lover he was, and while Logan was good in bed, the thought of someone new, the mystery and the unknown, was so tempting.

I had Jason's cell number. I didn't use it. As much as I wanted sex, I wanted sexual validation more. I didn't want to cheat, to hurt Logan. I wanted to look into someone's eyes—Logan's—and see desire again.

At first, I thought the knock I heard was on the door of the room next to mine. I jumped, but then I looked at the clock and saw that it was nearly two. No one was going to come stumbling to my room at two a.m. But when I lay back on my pillow, I heard it again. A little bit louder and more insistent. And definitely my door.

Heart in my throat, I slipped out of bed and padded to the door. A million things big and small went through my head as I crossed the room. None of them made any sense, but I was exhausted, and my brain and body were sort of in fight or flight mode then. My first thought was the kids. Something was wrong with one of the kids. Mia had been in a car accident. Jake had fallen down the steps. The dog got out. I talked myself down from the mom ledge, because if something had happened with the kids, I would have had a phone call. Not a two a.m. visitor. The kids were safe at home with my brother and his wife.

It had to be Logan. Something had happened to Logan. What if he had too much to drink and stepped off a curb and was hit by a car? What if he had alcohol poisoning? What if he had a heart attack? What if he was fucking Charlotte, and someone had seen them together and had come to tell me?

What if it was Jason?

I peeked through the peephole and slid the chain lock open. The light in the corridor was garish and bright, but I could see the pained expression on his face. He drew a deep breath, like he was going to launch into a tirade, and I steeled myself for whatever was about to come.

Rather than speak, he lifted his hands and cupped the back of his neck. I watched with interest as he paced a small, tight circle in the hall, and finally looked at me again.

"Let me in."

His gruff, tortured voice chased a violent shiver up my spine. My skin prickled with awareness under my sleeveless silk sleepshirt. Wondering what brought him back, why he had decided to show up here now, I stepped backward without a word. I waited, watching the emotions at war over his face. The desire and need. To stay. To go.

I thought I knew before what I wanted, but in that moment, I felt his uncertainty well up inside me. I wanted him to stay, to want me, to want to be here with me. I needed his attention, his affection. I needed his body inside mine, because I hadn't felt whole in so long.

But fear made me hesitate.

The fear of what tomorrow might bring.

When he finally stepped over the threshold into my room, I moved my hand to swipe over the wall and find a light switch. The door closed leaving us in total darkness, and his fingers wrapped around my wrist. He tugged it away from the wall and pulled me hard against him.

"Leave it off."

His lips were warm and soft on my neck, but his kisses were insistent and suggestive. I buried my face in his shoulder and breathed in the scent of his aftershave and stale cigarette smoke and even liquor and beer. Turning my face to his neck, I wrapped my arms around his shoulders.

Tomorrow might be hell. Liars were never concerned with the truth; if needed, they would embellish things and create their own narrative.

He backed me against the door, and the press of his cock at my middle reminded me of the girls in the bathroom at the bar. Should they do a sex tape? I shut the mom in me up and screamed a silent *yes, do it, live a little. Make him see you. Make him make it good for you.*

Fear had robbed me of enough through the years. I wanted to feel something that night. So, when he fumbled with the safety lock on the door, I knew he planned to stay, come whatever tomorrow might bring. When he hesitated, the darkness made me bold. His breath on my face, I leaned into him and kissed him.

His mouth was a drug that captivated me. Because he couldn't see me, I played at his lips. I licked them and flicked the center of his upper lip with the tip of my tongue. He ground his hips into me, and the press of his cock made me moan with need. He closed his lips around my tongue and swallowed the noise. The kiss was deep and slow and so wet and suggestive, I felt his heat between my legs.

I wanted more, more of the lazy, languid strokes, and I wanted his body moving inside mine with those same slow, deep strokes, but this night was a gift. I wanted to play, and I needed him to want the same thing. I turned my head to break the kiss, and in the darkness, we stood nearly mouth to mouth, out of breath but needing more.

Again, I outlined his lips with the tip of my tongue, but this time, I cupped his face in my hands to hold him still.

The scratch of his whiskers on my palms made me shiver again, anticipating that same scratching between my breasts and my thighs. To tease him, I slipped my tongue between his lips and touched the roof of his mouth behind his teeth. The low rumble of appreciation in his throat vibrated on my hands.

Kissing is so intensely personal and so fucking sexy when you do it right. He nipped at me then, his teeth tugged at my lower lip, and the stab of pleasure-pain rendered me weak in the knees. I hadn't been doing this right for so long. Grateful for the darkness so I could relearn my way around a man's body without feeling self-conscious, I dropped my head back to rest on the door and let him kiss me.

Pressed between his hard body and the door, with his mouth closed over mine, my oversensitive skin hurt for his touch. His hands slid down over my waist and cupped my ass cheeks, and his mouth on mine moved from gentle and giving to bold and demanding. I wanted to please him. I wanted to blow his fucking mind, to make him come hard and remember that it was me that made him feel like a king. When he nibbled a trail from my mouth to my ear, I turned my head enough to give him access.

He mumbled something, but with his teeth in my neck, I didn't know what he said. His hands gripping my ass painfully hard said more than any words could. Desperate to feel his cock in my center, to create friction on my clit, I lifted my leg. Understanding my need, without moving his hands from my ass, he gathered my gown in his fingers and tugged it up, so I could wrap my leg around his waist.

I gasped out loud when he rocked forward against me and his straining cock pressed on me. I needed more, needed to put my other leg around him, needed him naked and balls deep inside me. I wanted to lock my ankles at his back and buck against him and make him work to ride me. But he held me there at the door and tortured me with another long, lingering kiss and the tiniest, teasing rock of his hips against mine.

When he stroked the back of my leg, just under my ass, I wondered if he knew I was wet. My panties were soaked, and suddenly I was consumed by the need for him to kneel before me and lap at me with his tongue. I needed to come, the orgasm I'd given myself earlier paled when compared to how badly I needed him to do it now.

He moved, then, but not to let me lift my other leg. Rather, he moved one hand and caught my wrist and lifted it to trap against the door above my head. I wished for handcuffs, because I wanted to lie on the bed, cuffed there and open to him to do with as he pleased. One hand pinned over my head, I was still free to touch him. I dragged my free hand over his shoulder and the sleeve of his shirt, and then hooked my fingers in the waistband of his jeans.

Head bent over my shoulder now—I could feel his breath on my skin—he licked the strap of my sleepshirt. With his body still pressing me to the door, and his hand still holding mine captive, he caught the black strap in his teeth and eased it off my shoulder. His whiskers burned over my skin, but as if he knew, he came back for a second pass, and this time, he dropped sweet kisses there, and then his mouth was gone until suddenly he sank his teeth into my breast.

Through the silk, he laved my breast, and then he closed his teeth over my nipple and tugged, and the silk on my sensitive skin and his teeth tugging at me made me cry out. I worked one handed on his jeans, but I couldn't think to work his button. I gave up and cupped the length of his cock through the denim and reveled in his sharp intake of breath and the way he muttered fuck.

"Fuck me."

The quiet was different. No chattering. No music playing. The only sound was our heavy breathing, but I felt sexy there with my hand on his cock and him coming undone, and so I whispered to him over and over that I needed him to fuck me.

His grip loosened on my wrist over my head, and finally—praise God—he lifted my other leg to wrap around his waist. This time when he rocked forward, I moaned with the pleasure of having his full cock pressed tight to my center. I needed skin, though, so I hung onto his shoulders with one arm and guided my hand down between our bodies and into his jeans to touch him. His belly was hot against the back of my knuckles, and his shaft was hot and hard. I curled my fingers around him and smoothed the pad of my thumb over his head.

"Not yet," he growled, and I started to argue, to tell him I wanted to touch him. But he cupped my ass with one hand and slipped the fingers of his other hand inside my panties. The backs of his knuckles pressed against my clit as he rubbed the crotch of my panties in his fingers. The ache in my nipples was painful, and my pussy clenched with desperation. Finally, he turned his hand

and pumped his fingers inside me. His thumb moved in big, lazy circles over my clit.

"Yes." I hissed it as I moved with him, arching my back from the door and undulating my hips to ride his hand. He teased me, scissoring his fingers inside me and pressing harder on my clit only to draw back when he sensed that I might come.

"Do you wanna come?" His voice at my ear made me hotter, more desperate, and I moved faster, harder against his hand.

"Please," I whispered.

"Beg me." He tugged at my earlobe.

"Oh God, please. Please let me come."

Maybe it was the throb in my voice and maybe he wanted to fuck me with his cock, but he added another finger inside me and pressed hard and fast on my clit. I wished he could see me, because I cupped my breasts in my hands and rolled my nipples, and finally the electric heat rolled over me in wave after wave, and my body quivered as he continued to stroke me.

"Fuck me," I whispered against his mouth when he kissed me. "Take your clothes off and fuck me."

I was afraid he would say no. I had this sudden rush of fear that he had changed his mind. That he would drop a cool kiss on my cheek and wipe his fingers on my panties and slip back out the door as quickly and quietly as he had come in.

I gushed a deep sigh of relief when I felt him move and realized he was unbuttoning his shirt.

"Let me." Hungry for the heat in his skin, I pushed his hands away and with my legs still wrapped around his waist, I worked his buttons. My hands shook as I loosened the last one and then parted his shirt. I sculpted his hard shoulders as I shoved the material over them. When he shrugged out of it, I went to work on his jeans.

The trembling spread from my hands through my belly and down into my legs. Greedy for him, I pushed his jeans open and slipped my hand inside his briefs again. Desperate to own him, to possess his heart and soul, I cupped his balls and then gripped his shaft and tugged gently.

In the darkness, I heard the rustle of clothing and then his hands were everywhere at once. He tugged at the strap of my gown again, tearing it and pulling the silk from my body. The air was cool, but he dipped his head to kiss my neck. Hand still in his briefs, thumb smoothing circles over the crown of his cock, I closed my eyes and soaked up the warmth of his body pressed so close to mine. His soft hair on my chin and my neck as he eased his lips down my chest tickled and drew a shiver from deep and low in my spine.

His hands cupped my ass again as he nudged my nipple with his tongue.

"Now. Please."

The tug of his lips around my nipple sent a jolt of pleasure straight to my core. I moaned out loud and whispered again to take me now. He turned, my legs still wrapped around his waist, and carried me in the darkness toward the bed. With his shirt discarded by the door, his soft, warm skin on mine was a thrill. At the bedside, I slid my legs down over his and scooped my sleepshirt up over my head to drop on the floor. He turned away from me for a second to turn on a lamp. The warm, glowing light cast his face in shadow, but the heat in his eyes turned me on. Starved for that, for someone to need me like this, I smoothed my hands over his bare chest as he toed off his shoes and worked his jeans down his hips. He smelled and tasted like clean, red-blooded man, and I sank my teeth into him, scraping his nipple and then I went back to it to rub that tender skin with the flat of my tongue.

Ready to take him inside me and make him beg me, I mewled in protest when he fell to his knees in front of me. But like a man dying of thirst, he ignored me, and cupped my hips in his hands. The press of his nose against my panties rendered me weak, again, and I flailed my arms to find purchase. His fingers hooked the waistband of the silk and pulled the panties just low enough to bare my clit to him.

"Hold on."

That gruff command made my stomach and my pussy clench. I dropped my hands to his shoulders as he spread me open with his thumbs to lick me. He teased me with soft little strokes over my clit and inside me, his thumbs accidentally on purpose grazing me again and again.

"Please."

Gone was my need to possess him. I needed him to drive me over the edge again; I needed to explode. I wanted my face to tingle with pleasure, stars to cloud my vision. If he would break me first, I would possess him and be the only woman in the world.

His tongue changed from flicking to rubbing and then he sucked my clit into his mouth, grazing me with his teeth. Blind with desperation, I cupped the back of his head and pushed his face further into me. His hair was soft on my hand, and his mouth was hot and demanding.

"Come, Ava," he said into my sex as he plunged his

fingers inside me again. The orgasm rolled languidly from my toes to my hips to my fingertips. I sobbed out loud and squeezed my eyes closed; tears wet my face. He played, drawing that delicious, electric warmth over me again, and then his hands were in my panties again, pushing them to the floor.

"Look at me."

I did. I watched him slide up my body. I watched him flick his tongue in my belly button and close his teeth over my nipples, and then our bodies pressed together shoulders to hips. His briefs the only barrier between us now, I curled my arms around him to mold my breasts to his chest and hold him. My hands read his muscle movement through his skin, and I plunged both into his briefs to cup and squeeze his ass cheeks.

"Fuck me," I said again, and finally, he stripped the briefs off and stood nude before me, his cock thick and hard.

"Like this," he said, and he turned me and gave me a gentle nudge to the bed. On my knees, with my ass in the air, I looked at him over my shoulder, thrilled and aroused again when I saw the way his eyes roamed over my body. In one fluid motion, he leaned over to grab his jeans and pulled his wallet from the pocket. My body in flames, I watched him tear open a condom and roll it on.

Our eyes met as he gripped my hips and then spread me open again to look at me.

"Oh, yes. Please." I groaned, but a tiny sob of need slipped out when he rubbed his fingers over me again, clit to my ass. He drove into me hard, like he was desperate to feel my heat around his cock. Hands on the bed in front of me, I pushed back against him with each thrust, desperate to blow his mind.

Hard and fast, he fucked me, and he came with a sharp yell and a quick jerk of his hips, and I worked his cock to draw everything from him I could. Happy, exhausted, I wanted to collapse on the bed, but I arched my back and moaned softly when I felt his fingers between my legs again. When I came, the orgasm smaller and softer this time but no less pleasurable, I dropped to the bed to catch my breath. Afraid that he would leave then, that I would sleep alone, I closed my eyes and wished the tears away.

"Give me a minute." He pressed into me, his weight heavy on my back, and then he slipped to my side and threw his leg over mine.

Still scared that he would leave now that he'd had what he came for, I was silent. He worked his arm around my waist and up over my arm, above my head. He covered my hand with his and entwined his fingers with mine.

Safe for the first time in weeks, I closed my eyes and breathed in the scent of sex and alcohol and stale cigarette smoke.

CHAPTER 8

Logan

I shouldn't have followed Charlotte out of the bar. I knew it wasn't a good idea when I did it. I was a little bit wrecked. Not drunk, but I was feeling the effects of the liquor I had consumed. I was overwhelmed by things Charlotte had said—the personal stuff about her and Ross as well as the things she had suggested my wife might be thinking. I sat there for a few minutes trying to process all of it.

The shitty thing was that even after all of it, after Charlotte spoon fed me the things that Ava might be thinking and feeling, even after Charlotte casually mentioned that she and I had almost had a fling and then thrown that personal shit at me about her and Ross, I wanted to fuck her. Had nothing at all to do with my wife. With needing to get away from my wife. With wanting to leave her, to file for divorce. Honestly, my brain stalled on the image Charlotte had offered of Ross performing oral sex on her, and I finally tossed back the last of my scotch and left the bar looking for her.

I found her at the elevator, and maybe if our rooms had been on the top floor, we would have fucked each other then. There wasn't time for it, but we were alone in the car, and we were on each other before the doors were completely closed.

"What the fuck are you doing, McKinley?"

I'm too old to spend half a night drinking, I can tell you that. Garrett's voice was like a fucking jackhammer tearing into my eardrum and my head. And I knew he wasn't speaking loudly at all, because he was giving me the hairy eyeball and the dramatic cartoon scowl as if warning me to keep it down.

"Drank too much," I mumbled with a shrug. I popped a couple of aspirin and swallowed them with a gulp of water. "And I didn't sleep a lot. And I feel like shit."

"Where'd you go last night?" Garrett sidled up beside me at the breakfast table, which that day amounted to croissants and pastries, naturally, since a good old-fashioned greasy breakfast of bacon and eggs was what I needed.

I didn't want to talk about it. It hit me the night before that I should never have mentioned that Ava and I were having any issues. So, I took my ring off. Big deal. If anyone asked, I could have said I lost it. I was having it resized. Or maybe, if say, Garrett had mentioned it, then maybe I would have just told him. The way I handled it put Ava out there as a target for rumors, and it put our marriage under a microscope, and the advice, support—whatever the fuck you wanted to call it—was anything but helpful.

"Called it early," I hedged.

Garrett grabbed some kind of baked thing with apple slices and shaved almonds. He eyed me suspiciously as he tore off a big bite and lowered it to his saucer. Ignoring him, I leaned around him to study the offerings and decide if I was hungry enough to eat one.

"Bullshit." He talked with his mouth full. From the corner of my eye, I saw him wipe his mouth with a little cocktail napkin. Not a coffee drinker, he popped the top on a canned soda and took a long swig. "You left the bar with Charlotte."

"Charlotte and I walked back to the hotel together," I admitted. Too easy to catch me in that lie, so why not be honest? "We had a drink in the bar, talked for a bit, and called it a night."

"Yeah? And then what?" Garrett took another big bite of the pastry thing and waved the hand with the saucer in it at me. He nudged me in the chest as he chewed. "You didn't go to your room, man."

I did, but not right away. Uncomfortable with his interrogation, I looked over my shoulder at the growing crowd in the conference room. The cold fingers of fear gripped my heart when I saw Ava across the room. She sipped from a paper coffee cup as she spoke with Sherri Frank. I couldn't breathe for a second. In a black sweater dress and long black boots that covered her calves to her knees, she owned the room. She'd swept the side of her hair back to expose her ear, and from all the way across the room, I could see the diamond studs I gave her as an anniversary present nine years ago.

I stared too long, because Garrett caught me and turned to see what or who I was checking out. He finished chewing that bite, rubbed his fingers over his lips, and nodded as he turned back to me.

"That's what I'm talkin' about." He shrugged, eyes wide with disbelief, maybe. "You're so totally fucking things up with her. Ava's not dumb, Logan."

She's not. That he said so, that a male colleague said so puffed me up with pride, and then I imagined Charlotte slapping me and telling me to get over my fucking self. Why should a male colleague acknowledging my wife's intuition or sharp wit make me proud? I could stand there in that room and point out a hundred brilliant women. Hell yes, my wife was one of them, and it was me making her less than that. It was me making her someone other than the same as the rest of these people I respected.

I wondered if every other man in the room would do the same, or if I was the sole dick there that day.

"Let it go, Garrett," I said quietly as I turned back to the table. I grabbed a bagel, though not my favorite, as if by doing so, as if by choosing the least attractive baked good on the table, I was offering proof that I would never cheat on my wife.

"Not gonna let it go," he mumbled around another mouthful. "I'm not gonna stand by and watch you fuck up nineteen years. She's the better half of you, you know that."

"You ever cheat on Tricia?" I asked to shut him up, not as a prelude to a confession.

"Jesus God." He groaned and thumped his forehead. "Are you kidding me? You think it's not gonna be common knowledge by the end of the day that you fucked Charlotte Benz last night?"

"I didn't say that I did," I reminded him. "I'm asking you if you're faithful to Tricia."

"Yes. I am."

"Yeah? Even with all the flirting and pawing around?"

"Yes." He nodded. "There's not a woman out there who turns me on like my wife. I might have fun, McKinley, but I know where to draw the line."

The bagel was dry and cold, but I didn't want to take the time to toast it. I fought with a cold butter patty and finally gave up and took a bite. I hadn't seen Charlotte yet this morning, and I wanted to make sure she was okay. But I couldn't ask Garrett if he had seen her. Not after his tirade.

"Hey."

I shuddered when I heard Ava's voice right behind me.

"Hey, beautiful." Garrett hurried to swallow his last bite of the pastry so he could kiss my wife on the cheek. Up close, she was beautiful. Her eyes were bright, and her smile was warm. Until she turned to me. She toned it down a notch, from gushing and friendly to cautious and polite. Talk about a knife in the heart. Never thought I'd see the day she was happier to see Garrett than me.

"You guys over here staking a claim?" She curled her fingers around my arm and ducked in between us to get to the breakfast items. "I'm starving."

I eyed her hand on my arm, her nails filed and painted a muted gray, her fingers bare. It never crossed my mind when I took my wedding ring off that she would take hers off, too. I didn't like the look of her hand without it.

"Out late?" Garrett asked her. I wasn't sure if he was needling me or genuinely curious. "I bet you were out dancing, working up an appetite."

Ava snorted. "I haven't danced since my niece got married, Garrett. That was three years ago."

I opened my mouth to argue with her, because surely, she and I had danced together since then. But realizing we hadn't, I took a bite of the bagel and stood there like a fucking pansy while Garrett schmoozed my wife.

"Yeah? You were out though, right?"

Selection made, Ava moved to grab a saucer. I watched her hand slide away from me and just caught myself before yanking it back.

"Yeah." She shrugged as she turned back to us. The cream cheese pastry didn't surprise me. That I didn't grab one for her and take it to her almost gutted me. She took a bite and chewed silently for a moment. "Dinner with Madelyn and Jason. Went to some bar for drinks later."

"No dancing at the bar?"

"No. Not really up for it," she mumbled as she shot me a quick look. When our eyes met, electric heat shot through me. I reached up to tug at my tie only to remember I wasn't wearing one. Hadn't for years.

"Dinner was good, though?"

"It was." She nodded. "How about you guys?"

"Dinner and drinks." Garrett gave her the side eye and a smirk. "Yada yada yada."

"You love it, Garrett." She shrugged. "See you guys later."

"You fucking kidding me?" Garrett turned on me when Ava reached the far side of the room and sat down by Madelyn. "Your wife stands here to talk to us, and you said what to her? Nothing? Nothing, McKinley? Nineteen fucking years you guys have lived together, and this is what you boil down to?"

"Every conversation we have is a fight." It was a lame excuse, however true it was.

Garret huffed, clearly irritated with me.

"Just remember, Logan. You might be having some fun while you put your marriage on hold." He shrugged. "She might be, too. And we've already established that she's pretty smart. What happens when she realizes she doesn't need you?"

All true, and so reminiscent of what Charlotte said that I wanted to ask if they had compared notes. Instead, I tossed the rest of my bagel and excused myself to use the restroom before the session started.

Charlotte kisses like she has all the time in the world. Not lazy, but thoroughly. She licks and strokes and prefers open-ended and open-mouthed kisses. It's impossible not to look at her and wonder what it would be like with her. Sex. If she likes it hard and fast or if she demands a slow hand. In the elevator last night, one of those kisses drew a long, low moan from her lips, and the next day I still wondered if it was pleasure or need.

When I came back from the men's room, I found her seated next to my wife. Ava watched her talk, clearly interested, and I hated myself for what I had done. So, shit was happening at home. I was pissed off at Ava and pissed off at the kids and drained and looking at the grass on the other side of the fence and sure as hell, it looked greener over there.

I wondered what Ava was telling people about me.

I wondered if we were too far away from the people we had been when we fell in love to find each other again.

If I wanted to find her again.

Charlotte saw me when I took a seat next to Garrett.

She sort of shook her head at me, as if chastising me, but then she licked her lips like she wanted to turn me on. I dragged my eyes from her to my wife's crossed legs and imagined the way she locked her ankles over my ass when we fucked. The way we fit together like we were made for each other.

The session ran a little long, and I was in a rush to get to the next one. Garrett had a one-on-one sit down with someone, so I knew he wasn't headed where I was. Still, we walked out of the room together, and Travis Harms was with us.

Ava and Charlotte were walking at our side, but Ava didn't seem all that enthralled anymore by what Charlotte was saying. I wondered if Ava knew about Ross's work-related accident. If she knew Charlotte had been told she couldn't have children. Were they close enough to share that sort of stuff? Which led me right back to wondering if Ava had confided to anyone—Madelyn, maybe—about all the things that had broken in our marriage.

"I'm just sayin'." Garrett shrugged and gave me a helpless look. "I knocked on your door at three a.m. Logan. You weren't there."

I wasn't, but I had no intention of discussing it with him, especially not in a group of people who, like any group of people, would overhear us and repeat everything later.

"Everybody knows you're fuckin' around with Charlotte Benz."

Thankfully, the corridor had cleared out, but Ava and Charlotte were standing just ahead of us now. Charlotte had her head ducked over her phone as she scrolled through something. But Ava turned her head and met my eyes.

"I don't wanna spend a weekend helping you move your ass into a permanent new place," Garrett continued, unaware that Ava was watching and listening now. "I don't wanna listen to your stories about your weekend with the kids. I don't wanna watch your wife walk into a hotel with someone else." He shrugged, and as done as I was with his preaching, I got it. He was sincerely concerned for me and for Ava.

"I got it, Garrett," I promised him.

"I hope you do, man."

CHAPTER 9

Ava

He was gone when I woke up the next morning.

But we burned that damned hotel room up that night. We dozed, lying together sideways over the bed, and then he woke me with sweet, staccato kisses up my spine and the back of my neck. I had no idea what time it was, and I never stopped to think about the next day or the day after that. I turned over in his arms, and I held on.

The second time started with those same kisses. Short and sweet, cautious and curious, long and deep. Mouths and necks and arms and legs. The sweet, sexy spots. He drove me back to orgasm again, and when I had wiped away the tears the second time, I shimmied down his body in the warm glow of the lamp and took his cock in my mouth.

Hands in my hair, he guided me for a moment, showing me how to take him. I licked him from his balls to the head of his cock, and I closed my lips around his shaft and sucked him until he cried out and jerked his hips from the bed. He moved his hands from my hair and linked our fingers, and then he flipped me over and kissed me again.

When my alarm went off at seven and I turned my head to where he had slept only to find him gone, I worried it was all a dream. But my body ached in places I hadn't used for a while, and I was nude beneath the sheet and the comforter.

One perfect night of sex.

But with daylight I was back to being alone. The tears that I left on the pillow he'd slept on weren't a physical release. They weren't an involuntary response to extreme physical pleasure. They were an expression of my sadness, of how alone I felt again.

A hot shower soothed the tender aches, though the water made my skin sting where he'd left whisker burn. I wanted to pack my bags and go home, to see the kids, to find comfort in the familiar. But when I toweled off and stared at my reflection in the mirror, I thought of the night before. Not just about my pleasure, but his need to give it to me. My need to own him, and his explosive orgasms. He rendered me powerless and desperate, but he needed to own me as badly as I needed him. I had delivered mind-blowing pleasure to him, too.

Rather than slink home, I felt empowered, so I took extra time with my appearance. I wanted him to see me again today. I wanted every man there to see me, as a woman and as their equal, and I wanted every woman to know I was on her side. The hot coffee from the café in the hotel did wonders for me, and it wasn't until I stepped into the conference room and lit eyes on everyone—on

Charlotte and Jason and Garrett and Logan—that my confidence, my energy, flagged a bit.

I spent a few minutes mingling, as everyone does before a session. So much of our travel is educational, yes, but the networking is sacred, so talking to Sherrie Frank and Madelyn and Jason about business was important. Necessary. But I was hungry, and I finally braved the guardians at the food table. I wasn't up for seeing Garrett any more than I knew what to say to Logan, but I figured people were watching, and I was loathe to cause a scene.

Garrett seemed sincere when he greeted me. Don't get me wrong. I like the guy; I guess it's just seeing him with double vision that makes it hard. He's good on the job; and he's kind-hearted and fun-loving. But not only am I a businesswoman, I'm a wife, and he doesn't always look great through that lens.

It didn't escape me that my husband didn't say a word to me. I touched him. I clutched his arm as I moved by them to grab a pastry. I hoped it looked casual, but it wasn't. It was me staking a claim on him, because I still worried about Charlotte. Odds are, if we end up divorced, even with all the other mess in our lives, in my heart, I'll blame Charlotte. And if we reconcile, which seems impossible if we don't communicate, I'll still always wonder about Charlotte and what Logan shared with her.

After the session, I had a meeting scheduled with a rep from The Christianson Group. Charlotte had claimed a chair by me before the session, and we talked a bit, and while I liked her and always had, there was a sliver of my heart and my brain that hated her. She seemed a little sad, and she mentioned that Ross was still struggling with the back injury. Maybe if I were a better friend I would have asked more and been more concerned.

When we filed out of the conference room, she was talking about throwing darts at a bar the night before. Someone missed the dart board but hit a customer passing through. Might have been funny, but we were near enough to Garrett and Logan that I could hear their conversation.

Garrett sounded put out by Logan's behavior, and I wondered what he knew. What Logan had done to make him so angry. I wouldn't ask. Logan had moved out, but we were still married, and his need for space scared the hell out of me. I wanted to know everything. I had the right to know everything. But I knew I wasn't strong enough to hear it, to accept the things Logan had done and forgive him if he came back to me.

There were a couple of guys in the café this morning waiting for their orders. I overheard them; Logan and Charlotte were the talk of the weekend. According to those guys—pretty sure one was Pete Martin from Omaha, but I had no idea who the other guy was—Logan had spent the night with Charlotte last night.

The only reason I could stomach talking to Charlotte this morning, that I could lift my head and look my husband in the eyes when Garrett made that comment to him after the session, was that I knew without a doubt he didn't spend the night with her.

It was all I knew without question.

He didn't hold eye contact with me for long, and I found that particularly damning. When he looked away, I turned to Charlotte. She stared at me silently for a moment, and I waited for her to deny it. That she didn't, that she didn't say a word, bothered me.

It's hard to walk through your day, out in the real world, when your husband is part of that every day real world, and you have these crazy issues hanging between you, and your life is further complicated with liars and rumors. Maybe I'm a liar, too, because I was pretending to be okay. Maybe that made me the biggest liar of all.

Or maybe that was Logan.

Logan who found fault with me for babying our son and being irritated with his collections and questioning his search for the fountain of youth and Logan who maybe was fucking another woman.

Thank God, the Philadelphia trip wrapped up that evening, though finding Jason and Madelyn at our gate at the airport the next morning was less than pleasant. Logan carried on a lively conversation with the cab driver on the way from the hotel to the airport, but he seemed genuinely challenged to think of a thing to say to me. He and Jason settled in at the gate and talked about data speed and threw in bits about Nascar and NFL, and Madelyn flipped through a magazine.

I watched Logan with Jason and for a moment found myself hating them both.

Men.

For their puffed up, peacock strutting bullshit. Why couldn't they just be themselves? Why couldn't Logan just be himself, my husband, my kids' dad? When had he decided it wasn't enough for him, and what could I ever do about how he felt?

When we boarded, I held my breath, praying that Jason and Madelyn found seats somewhere else. And then

I held my breath when they did, and Logan and I were seated side by side and an elderly Asian woman sat at my other side.

"Have you heard from the kids?" he asked as people continued to file through the aisle, looking for a seat.

I stared at him silently for a moment and finally shook my head and looked away.

"What?" He sighed loudly to let me know he was put out by my pissy attitude already.

"That's all you have to say to me? Really?"

It still hurt. My heart hurt, and if Logan was really moving through the process of leaving me, I had a hell of a long way to go to feel better. But that morning, the tears were gone, and my voice was hard and cool with anger.

"What am I supposed to say?"

"I don't know, Logan." I shrugged. "But if you can't figure it out after nineteen years, then maybe we are done."

He huffed out another long-suffering sigh and dropped his head back on the seat. I peeked at him to find his eyes closed and his mouth in a hard line.

"It was the lipstick," he admitted.

I flinched and swung my gaze the other way. The lipstick that I grabbed at the grocery store the other day, before we left for Philadelphia. Not even a high dollar brand. My husband could be turned on by dime store red.

He reached his hand over my lap and took my hand, but I snatched it away from him, careful not to bump the woman beside me. I turned to him and leaned close, pressed my lips to his ear as if to kiss him.

"You put on a condom to fuck your wife," I whispered. "And you were gone when I woke up."

CHAPTER 10

LOGAN

Ava's frosty tone hurt worse than if she had bit my ear there on the plane. She was right—using a condom the other night had been a mistake—but crammed into a metal tube ready to climb to cruising altitude and spend a few hours with her and a hundred other people didn't seem like a good time or place to get into it.

I wasn't thinking when I took that condom from my wallet, but then, really? Ava had come undone at my hands the second she let me into the room, and the dirty words and the way her voice got all thick and husky when she was turned on had me ready to blow. Perched on all fours with her gorgeous ass in the air, I didn't take a second to think about what it would look like when I put the condom on.

On the flight, I took her hand again, willing her to understand that this was me, trying. That I wanted to fix it. She didn't make a scene, but she didn't curl her fingers around mine the way she used to. The relief on her face when the flight attendant came by offering snacks that she *had* to take with that hand, of course, cut me. I took the bag of pretzels as a consolation prize and then leaned away from her in my seat, folded my arms over my chest, and pouted the rest of the flight.

Her silent treatment has some serious teeth, and I figured if I looked over my body, I would find bite marks. Other than the ones she had left there the night in the hotel room. I couldn't think too much about that night because remembering the way she touched me in the dark, and remembering her voice begging me to fuck her made me so fucking hard, it hurt.

My apartment felt cold and empty when I got home, so I found reasons to go by the house a few nights in a row. I fixed the leaky faucet finally and ignored her when she expressed wonder at how little time it took me once I actually did it. I took Jake and Mia out for pizza one night, and I asked Ava to go with us. With a cool, clipped tone, she shot me a quick, dismissive glance and said she couldn't. She had things to do. I would have argued, I might have begged, but both Jake and Mia were watching us, so I rounded the kids up and left her home alone.

To do her things.

I think something happened in Philadelphia. Something other than the stuff with me and Charlotte in the elevator. And other than me and Ava fucking like animals in her hotel room. I'm not sure what, but something feels different. Yeah, Charlotte's take on the whole thing, Charlotte's personal revelations were uncomfortable, and her spinning them to Ava, suggesting Ava might feel as she did now and then totally blew my mind.

But it felt like more than that. I hadn't heard any

rumblings, no rumors. Yeah, I know Ava was hanging around Jason Smith that trip, but I hadn't heard anything suggesting something happened between them. And I trusted her.

Mostly.

Still, Ava walked out of that hotel the morning we flew home a different woman than when we checked in. And while it was intriguing, it was also terrifying.

Travel usually wrapped up for us with a final trip to New York in late November or early December. I didn't want to go. Or, maybe more accurately, I didn't want Ava to go if I went. I wasn't sure why, and believe me, in those long hours I spent alone at my apartment, I thought of little else. I still found Charlotte attractive, but after that night of dirty, hardcore sex with Ava, I didn't need Charlotte's affection or mutual attraction. I loved the woman, but in an entirely different way than I loved Ava, and I had no illusions that if Ava and I split up permanently Charlotte and I would be a thing.

I didn't want anything more than the friendship I had with Charlotte.

Maybe I wanted *less* than the friendship and the dicking around we'd been doing.

After that heart to heart with Charlotte—well, no, she had my balls in a vise while she read me the riot act, actually—I didn't want my wife out there. I had this insane Neanderthal reaction that I wanted to keep her at home. Private for me and only me. I'm not sure I worried that she would fuck around on me, though I sure considered the possibility after what Charlotte said. But I also didn't want to think that somewhere in Philadelphia that night, my wife was sitting across a cocktail table with a knife to another man's balls, airing our dirty laundry to prove a point to him.

And it wasn't that I was worried about the dirty laundry itself, because yes, I had fucked up to begin with when I took my ring off and told the table at large in Dallas that we were having issues. It was more the idea that while Ava might not crawl into bed and spread her legs for another man, I had learned there were a lot of ways to be deeply intimate and even dirty with a woman that could happen in a bar, when you were fully clothed.

I didn't want Ava to be *one of the guys*. I didn't want Ava to tell someone else that I couldn't get it up for her anymore, but I could lick her to orgasm most nights, so it worked out. I didn't want to think of my wife telling a colleague whom I might see in a session the next morning that even though there was a lot more going on in our marriage with the kids and the dog and the car and the house, that when we were apart, everything wrong boiled down to fear that I didn't love her anymore.

I didn't want Ava on the road where she might look at another man and cry to him because of something I had done to her.

Mia asked me about Christmas that night I took the kids out for pizza. Would I come back for Christmas? What about dinner at Ava's brother's house on Christmas Eve? What about the four of us watching *The Santa Clause* together when we were back at home, curled up together in the living room before we went to bed? What about Christmas morning? Ava always made the coffee and cinnamon rolls, and I fried bacon and eggs, and the kids marveled at their haul while we ate.

I'm sure Mia—maybe Jake, too—was worried about

presents. They're kids, and even if their family life was spinning out of control, they wanted presents. But her sad face was about the traditions we'd built as a family. Maybe Jake didn't think about it, but Mia was definitely at the age when she had to worry Ava and I could end up divorced.

Mia's questions made me wonder if Ava had done anything to prepare for the holidays. Most years, we did some of the shopping together. But true to form, Ava often took care of the little things. The specific scarf or sweater Mia had asked for or making sure that Jake had the exact set of baseball cards or the correct game for the correct console. Ava wrapped all the gifts, and each one was done with care, with ribbons and bows and her neat handwriting on the tags.

Since I wasn't living there now, I wasn't privy to anything she was doing. Before Philadelphia, she was wrecked, and I spent my days angry that I had to feel guilty for taking a little step back to think about our marriage and what I needed from her, from our relationship. I don't know if she functioned at home without me around, and yeah, I know that sounds conceited. Which is why I'm making a big deal out of the fact that after Philadelphia, she was different.

The week before the New York trip, I dropped by on the pretense that I was checking the house to make sure it was winterized. Honestly, I don't even know what the fuck that means. But I could poke around the windows and doors and make sure the house was tight and no air was coming in anywhere. I could check the furnace filter. Make sure the faucet wasn't leaking again.

If it meant I could see Ava and size things up, I could do any of that.

And if it didn't go well, I needed more clothes and maybe a few movies and books to take back to my apartment.

I timed it to catch her alone. Mia had told me she had some kind of study group at her friend's house, and Jake was at basketball practice. The door was locked, but I still had a key, so I let myself in. The first thing I noticed—I think every fucking light in the house was on—set me off, but I clamped my mouth shut so tight, it hurt my teeth. The TV was on; Ava was watching a Christmas movie on one of those cable channels. They drove me fucking nuts, and she and I had fought about it on more than one occasion. How could she watch the same damned movie over and over—even when they were different, they were the same—and I would suggest watching something new or ask her if I could watch the football game. Most of the time she reminded me that we have four big screen TVs in the house, and then she'd jab me with the fact that I had recently been shopping for another one, and she would ask why I couldn't go downstairs to my mancave to watch whatever it was I needed to watch.

I hated the way she said mancave. With disdain. Total bitch mode. By that time, I would be so angry with her, I was happy to go downstairs where we do have a bar and a few TVs and a pool table. Ava drinks at that bar, watches those TVs, and shoots pool like a pro, but it's my mancave when she doesn't want me around upstairs.

Sometimes, when we got home from work, I broke my neck to get to the remote first, and I would tune into the poker channel and refuse to change it, just to piss her off.

"What're you doing here?" she asked that night. She had been in the dining room and had only stepped out to peek at the TV. I guess maybe she thought Alice was going to dare to be different and run off with the CEO of a multinational corporation that was sucking the economy of some third world country dry rather than stay in small town Bakersville and marry the drop-dead gorgeous and goodhearted carpenter who made nickels compared to the CEO.

I opened my mouth to answer her, but I was already angry, and I didn't want to pick a fight. Not yet. I would save it for later, pull the anger out for defensive moves if she attacked me.

"Thought we could talk."

Dressed in black yoga pants and an oversized red tunic, she was far from the sexy-as-fuck woman I had backed up against a hotel room door and fingered to make her come. But her hair had grown some, and she had some of it pulled back in a short, loose ponytail. No makeup, her skin looked rosy and sweet, like she was aging backwards.

She looked comfortable and approachable, like my wife.

And still, I wondered what kind of panties she was wearing, and I wanted to fuck her.

"Really." She mumbled the word, but I heard the sarcasm loud and clear.

"What?" I tossed my hands up, forgetting that I was going to hold onto my anger a little bit longer. "What does that mean? Don't we need to talk?"

She sighed and dropped her chin to her chest. I watched her ringless fingers knead the back of her neck, and it hit me again that this could happen. We were both so angry. At each other. At ourselves. At the kids. Life. It didn't matter that we loved each other; we were in a different phase of marriage, and I wondered how the hell we had come to be there. Staring at divorce.

And what to do about it. How to put the brakes on and stop the train wreck we were headed for.

"Sure." She nodded. She started to go back to the dining room, so I fell into step behind her. "Do you want a beer?" When she stopped abruptly, I ran into her and grabbed her by the sides to steady her. She whipped her head around, the ends of her hair grazing my face. I sank my fingers into her sides a bit harder and took a deep breath. The familiar scent of her lotion and her perfume made my heart hurt.

"Ava."

She shook her head violently and stepped around me to go back to the kitchen.

"Because I do." She avoided my eyes and then stood for a moment staring into the refrigerator.

"Yeah, that'd be good." I nodded. But she only pulled one longneck out and handed it to me.

"I think I need something stronger," she mumbled as she took a glass tumbler from the cabinet. I watched her pour a shot of bourbon in the glass. Behind us, the sound on the TV swelled with Christmas music, which probably meant it was the part where all the children in the small town gathered to sing "Frosty the Snowman." I was more interested in the woman in front me sipping the whiskey than if Alice and Jack saved Christmas and each other on screen.

"What do you wanna talk about, Logan?" Her whisper

was thick with emotion, but her eyes were dry when she turned to face me. She leaned on the counter at her back and folded one arm over her chest.

"What're we doing?"

"For Christmas?" She shrugged and sipped again.

"Goddammit, Ava. Don't do this."

She shook her head, sipped again, and then lifted the hand holding the glass to shut me up.

"Don't you fucking dare waltz in here and preach to me about our future."

"It's time to figure some things out."

"Oh, it's way past time to figure things out." Still whispering. Still dry-eyed.

"Why are you so angry? Right now. Why are you angry right now?"

"Maybe because it's been two weeks since you came to me in Philadelphia and fucked me brainless and then slipped out in the middle of the night and left me alone and haven't spoken to me about it since then." She pressed her lips together and eyed me curiously. "I don't know. What do you think, Logan?"

"It's not like we can drag this out and talk about it in front of the kids."

Her sharp, sarcastic snort hit me in the pride.

"What the fuck do you want me to do, Ava? I know you wouldn't touch this if the kids were anywhere around, so I'm here now, and you're gonna stand there and blow it off when we have the time to talk?"

She sniffled—the first sign that she might break, that she was hurting—and held the glass at her lips for a second before lowering it without drinking.

"Maybe you could tell me why you needed a condom to fuck me?" She cleared her throat. "Is that a good place to start?"

Of course, it was, but that didn't mean I was ready to face that whole issue. That I knew what to say as I squirmed under her heated glare.

"Okay, if you don't wanna start there, maybe you could tell me why you let Garrett, I.E. every other fucking person we know, believe that you were with Charlotte Benz that night, instead of just telling him you were with me?"

"I wanted to save you the embarrassment—"

"Save—?" She flinched, but her eyebrows jumped in surprise. "Save me the embarrassment? Of being with my husband? Why would you suddenly concern yourself with how I felt anyway?"

"What goes on between us is our business. I didn't think everybody at the RevTec event needed a visual of what you and I did in that hotel room."

"And yet you aired our personal business the day after you took off your wedding ring."

"I didn't tell anyone anything other than you and I were working through some issues."

"That's personal," she reminded me.

"Ava."

"Okay." She nodded and straightened. I followed her to the dining room, holding the beer I no longer wanted. I shouldn't have worried about Christmas gifts; the table was piled high with things for the kids and nieces and nephews and our parents. Ava had been in prep mode when I got here; she was checking her list to make sure no one was forgotten so she could start wrapping gifts. I felt a pang of guilt; there was no tree up—though to be fair, it was early—and she was alone doing something that should have been festive and fun.

"So." She dabbed at her eyes and eyeballed the table, probably expecting me to launch into my yearly lecture about overspending for the holidays. "Maybe you could tell me why you carry condoms around in your wallet. And why it was necessary to use them when we were together."

"We're separated," I mumbled, but it was a dumbass pansy thing to say, and I knew it. Ava glanced at me but said nothing.

"Look, Ava." I groaned. "Things are a mess, and yes, a lot of it is my fault, and yes, I had condoms in my wallet. But no, I have not been with another woman."

"You know." She sniffled again, but this time, she avoided looking at me. "I know you're attracted to her. I know you have been for a long time. But when people started talking about it, I didn't ask."

"Ava."

She lowered herself slowly to perch on the edge of a chair and propped her forehead in her hand.

"Not because I trusted you, Logan." She pursed her lips for a moment and finally rolled her head just enough to peek at me. "Because I didn't. And I was scared of what you would tell me."

To hear my wife say she didn't trust me gutted me. But in the next breath, the guilt—knowing how close Charlotte and I had come to crossing that line—filled me and made me want to puke.

"I was afraid that if I acknowledged that you wanted

out, that you wanted to be with another woman, you would take it as permission to go."

I didn't know what to say so I paced a circle around the table, careful to keep plenty of space between us. I was pissed that she didn't trust me, but I didn't trust myself much, either, and the things I'd done would hurt her if she knew about them.

"What is it about Charlotte?" Her voice was gruff, so she cleared her throat. "I mean, I liked her. Until I realized you were into her. But what do you see in her?"

"This isn't—" I started and stopped. Sucked in a deep breath and huffed it out, still frustrated and angry and lost as to how to fix everything we had broken. I felt Ava's eyes on me as I stood at the bay window and stared out into the darkness. "This isn't about Charlotte. It's not about anyone else. It's not about cheating."

"Maybe it's not to you." She shrugged. "I know we've got so much more than that to deal with, Logan. But you moved out, and you're looking outside our marriage for that...I don't even know...for intimacy. For release. For love." She set the whiskey tumbler on the table and rubbed her eyes. "If you're searching for someone else to give you any of that, it's about cheating."

"I haven't—"

"It would have been bad enough if you weren't actively looking, fucking someone else. Your public statement with your ring and moving out and flat out telling people we're having problems hurt me. You did that on your own. We should have discussed all of it, and instead, you took control of that and threw me under a bus with our friends and business colleagues."

"That wasn't my intention."

"You stripped me of my pride." She took a deep breath and shook her head. "As angry as I am with you, as much as you hurt me, I wouldn't do that to you." She turned to look up at me. "That's not fair."

"I'm sorry." Both of us could throw out a decent apology over simple things. If I forgot to pick up milk on the way home or if she shrunk a new shirt in the dryer, those were easy I'm-sorry things. But this was harder. Knowing how badly I hurt her—I never thought of what I did as taking a shot at her pride or aligning people on my side—made my gut burn with guilt. Knowing what I had done with Charlotte made me feel shameful. Both of those things only fueled my anger.

"Don't lie to me now."

"But no matter what, Ava, the problems started here. The constant fighting. We can't communicate, anymore."

"Did you fuck her then? Years ago?"

"No."

She sighed and watched as I moved back around the table to sit across from her.

"I kissed her one night." Just admitting that much, telling my wife that I had my mouth intimately pressed to another woman's was excruciating. "Then."

Her silent stare let me know she didn't believe me.

"What about Philadelphia?"

Garrett and a handful of other friends had seen me leave the bar with Charlotte. Other people had seen us together in the hotel bar. It was possible someone had seen us get on the elevator together and assumed we messed around there. Or that I did go to her room.

I nodded.

"Did you fuck her?"

"No."

"When?"

"The night I came to you."

"Jesus." She flinched. "Did you come right to me after being with her?"

"No, actually. We were in the elevator. Kissed her goodnight. She got off on her floor, and I went back down to the bar for another drink."

"Why?"

I twisted the bottle on the table, uncomfortable under Ava's guarded stare.

"I don't know. I was angry. At the world. At you. At myself. At Charlotte."

"She told you no?"

"No. But she said other things. She suggested I watch my step because you're not stupid. And because you're beautiful, and you were alone."

Ava snorted. "So, you came to me to stake your claim."

"I came to you because I wanted you."

"I wanted to break you that night, Logan." She pursed her lips and drew in a deep breath. Her nostrils flared, and her eyes filled with tears when they met mine. "I wanted to possess you. I wanted to be the only woman in your world."

I started to tell her she did; she succeeded, but she cut me off with a shake of her head.

"Instead, you reminded me that nothing's right. Nothing's fixed for us."

"Which is why—"

"And maybe it never will be."

Her whisper hammered me between the eyes.

As if she was unaware that she'd just yanked the rug out from beneath me, she sighed and looked at her watch.

"I have to go get Jake from practice."

"Do you want me to pick him up?"

"No." She shook her head. "I can do it, Logan. I always do."

CHAPTER 11

Ava

Logan was right. It wasn't as simple as cheating. Somewhere in the last few years, we had lost that connection. We were still there in the house, in the marriage, but we weren't Logan and Ava anymore. Being alone in our house, alone in our bed, gave me plenty of time to think about the way real life had eroded our relationship. It was a lot of little things that added up to this bigger thing and that bigger thing. It was all of the stupid little fights about me picking up after him or me not having dinner ready when he walked in from a late meeting. It was the familiarity, the very intimate things we saw in each other that weren't particularly sexy. Logan's tendency to leave pee spots on the tile in front of the toilet, me complaining of cramps or not shaving my legs every day the way I had when we first started sleeping together. The night his mom and I argued about whether or not Jake should be involved in school sports if he was struggling with his grades, the fact that while Logan didn't side with his mom, he didn't have my back, either.

No question that crazy, wild falling-in-love feeling is incredible. That free-fall giddy anticipation of seeing that person who makes your heart flutter. Everything's bigger and brighter and more fun in those early stages. There's never enough time to be together, to go places and hold hands and snuggle and make love. When Logan and I were younger, when we first started dating, I felt sorry for people who were alone, and I didn't get women—friends and co-workers—who didn't want relationships or marriage.

I can't pinpoint the moment all of that changed. And it wasn't like we just blew up overnight; we didn't go from being that crazy-in-love young couple to being passive aggressive or flat out aggressively attacking each other. We evolved into the middle-aged couple who sometimes chose a quick dinner out compared to a fancy, romantic dinner and a movie for a date night. There were times we snuggled all night, spooned, rather than fucked. And no question, the dirty, fast sex between us became deeper and slower and quieter with kids in the house. Even then, we endured the kids' moans and groans about it when the door was closed, and they knew we were doing stuff they thought was gross.

Finally, we had stepped into the phase of marriage that challenged our commitment. It stopped being easy to love. It was time to put work, effort, into the relationship or admit defeat and walk away. And that's where it felt to me like it was as simple as cheating. One night, Logan and I had a knock down drag out, and the next day he took his ring off. The fight started about the damned dog—the dog had been a fight to begin with, because I didn't want a dog, and I sure as hell hadn't expected him to bring home a German Shepherd—and the dog supposedly biting a kid in the neighborhood. As much as I wasn't a Charlie fan, I didn't think he would hurt a fly. But immediately, Logan started ragging on Jake; it was Jake's fault that Charlie got out. And if it was Jake's fault, that meant it was my fault, because Logan says I baby him. That I walk behind him and sweep up all of his messes which means I'm not allowing him to learn responsibility. Never mind the time that Mia was suspended for bullying a girl in her class and Logan went postal on her teacher and principal.

We talked about it. The night of the dog fight—I'm not sure a real dogfight could have been any uglier—we talked about separating. If it was the right thing to do. How it would affect the kids. I'm not sure that we calmed down enough to talk, so much as we had exhausted ourselves and each other, but we sat in the bedroom—on the floor, propped against opposite walls—and wondered what to do. How to fix it. If we simply needed space. Neither of us said *I'm sorry*. And neither of us said *I love you*.

It was the next day, when we were packing for Dallas, that I realized he had taken his ring off. It was in Dallas that he announced we were having issues. And then, there was Charlotte.

Which is what made it feel a whole lot like cheating was a huge part of our problem. We were at a point in our marriage where we had to decide together to make it work, to learn to communicate again, or end it and save the kids the ridiculous tension in the house.

And Logan chose personal space and Charlotte Benz to help him through our problems.

If he had only kissed her, I would still be angry. Jealous. And yes, I'm aware that I am guilty of the same now. I had kissed another man goodnight, and I had no romantic feelings for him at all. But we had a moment in that hotel hallway. It was an intimate moment, when our eyes met, and he touched part of me only my husband should touch, and everything we wanted to do together was right there between us. I don't feel guilty for it, because it didn't happen. Jason happened to be the man standing there with me, but it was Logan I wanted to be with. Conversely, knowing that Logan and Charlotte have apparently had multiple moments like that—for the record, I don't believe that's all that happened between them—burns me up inside with furious, mean jealousy.

Unfair of me, yes, but it's how I felt.

I suspected Logan would feel the same if he knew about the kiss between Jason and me.

Christmas had become just another thing on my to-do list. Logan would ask what I was getting for the kids, and he seemed interested in my answers though quick to frown about the money spent and the way I spoiled them. He would panic that we had forgotten to mail Christmas cards or to buy gifts for his parents. When I promised him it was all taken care of, he would nod and go on about his day, until eventually I felt like a puppy getting that small nod of praise.

I handled Christmas while he was living in the apartment. He did come over to help put the tree up. I left him and the kids to it, and I locked myself away in our office, working on emails and making a few phone calls. Still, listening to the Christmas music playing and Logan teasing and laughing with the kids hurt. I didn't know I was crying until I noticed wet spots on the desk calendar. He put the tree up and made sure the lights were on and working. I ducked my head and hid my eyes when he peeked in to tell me goodnight. But after everything we'd been through together, he knew me well enough to know I was crying.

"Ava."

I huffed out a quick, sharp breath and looked up at him, praying I could control the tears. I should have asked him to stay to help with the rest of it. Putting the ornaments on the branches. Making sure the tree skirt was straight. Laying out all the packages I had already wrapped. But I didn't. I wanted him to go back to his apartment alone and be as lonely there as I was here in our house.

I shook my head and pressed my lips together. Refused to speak. I ignored that little voice inside my head that kept whispering I was making a mistake. I was pushing him away, right into someone else's arms and life.

Charlie hovered near him there in the doorway of the office. I almost told him to take the damned dog, just because it felt like a good dig, since it was the damned dog that had blown the hole in our marriage wide open. But the kids loved Charlie, too, and they were already missing out on time with their dad. I couldn't banish the damned dog and make this any harder than it already was.

"Are you going to New York?"

Filled from head to toe with bitterness and sadness and just plain old pain, the laugh that slipped out of my mouth was harsh and sharp. Tears on my face—thank God, I had found a waterproof mascara since Logan had left me—I tipped my head and watched him with a frown.

"Why wouldn't I be going to New York?"

He looked around the office as if he might find an answer on the desk or the bookcase at the back wall.

"I dunno."

"Because you don't want me around." I shrugged. "Right?"

I expected him to argue with me. To say of course he wanted me around. If not for him, I thought he would at least acknowledge that I'm good at what I do, and other people in our industry respected me, even if he didn't.

"No." He shook his head. "I don't."

His answer was a knife in my heart. I blinked at him, stunned that he had said it. I couldn't breathe; that knife was lodged so deep, I was paralyzed. If he plunged it harder, I would die. If he tried to backstep now and pull it out, I would bleed out.

"Jesus, Logan." I buried my face in my hands and rubbed my eyes.

"Charlotte—"

"No." The word was hollow. It tore up my throat and out of my mouth. "No. I get it. You made your choice—"

"I didn't make my choice!" Logan bellowed. I didn't even care at the moment that the kids were in the living room. That they could hear every word he said, if not what I said, too, with the door open now. I wanted to throw something at him, after the speech he had given me the other night about never cheating. I actually looked around the desktop for something to heave at him, because I was hurt and humiliated, and I wanted him to hurt just a fraction of the way he hurt me.

"Here's the thing." I sniffled and swallowed hard. "She doesn't know you like I do, Logan. So, she might be into you for a time or two. But whatever you guys have will burn out. It'll fade away just like we did—"

"I don't want to ever think about you sitting in a bar with someone—someone we both know—telling him the things she told me. I don't want to lose you to someone who sees you as one of the guys, but even better, because you've got a great rack. I don't wanna lose our intimacy to something cheap and fake—"

"Like you and Charlotte?"

"There's nothing between me and Charlotte."

"Tell it to someone else, Logan. I don't believe you."

"How are we ever gonna make this work? How are we ever gonna get to the heart of you and me when you keep dragging her into it?"

"I've never dragged her anywhere," I whispered. "I just can't pretend like I don't see the way you feel about her."

"This is ridiculous." He groaned and stalked across the room to stand by my desk.

"I thought..." I hesitated but saw that he was watching me with a pained expression and continued. "I thought when you came to me that night in Philadelphia, it was over. That the end of us was over, and you were coming back. I thought it meant that you loved me."

"Ava." Logan leaned over and dropped his hands to the desk to lean. "I do."

"Then why did you not tell Garrett it was me that you were with? And don't tell me you were saving me."

"What does that mean?"

"*You* were saving face. You wanted him...you want them all to think you're some hotshot who can keep his wife in the dark and handle a side piece. You want them all to think you're getting a piece of Charlotte Benz. And—"

"No."

"And," I said louder, "if you were trying to save me, it's that you know everyone we talk to thinks you're fucking her, and if you said it was me, they wouldn't believe you. They would think you were lying to protect me. And that maybe I'm pathetic enough that I would have your back in that lie."

"That's the stupidest thing I've ever heard."

"Get out."

"Do you love me?" Still leaning over the desk, he stared at me with his intense blue eyes long enough to make me squirm. "Do you still love me, Ava? Because sometimes I wonder."

"I do." I nodded. But I closed my eyes and turned my face away from him. "But sometimes I wish I didn't."

CHAPTER 12

Logan

We rode to the airport together, but I didn't sit by her on the plane. I know that makes me look like a total dick, but I couldn't do it. Not after that last big blow up. Not after she continued to drag Charlotte into the middle of everything when she knew as well as I did that Charlotte and what happened or almost happened was the result of our problems, not the cause of our problems. I argued with myself for days leading up to the flight. Told myself just to suck it up and sit by her. So, we would sit there and stare at our iPads or pretend to sleep, or whatever, but we didn't have to talk.

But as I followed her down the aisle of the plane, I watched her drop into a seat next to a girl who didn't look much older than Mia, which would have left me the aisle seat. Perfect. But when Ava looked up at me from her seat, I remembered standing over her in the office the other night and asking if she loved me.

I wish I didn't.

That hurt worse than if she had said no, she didn't have feelings for me anymore. Knowing that she loved me but didn't want to made me see red. I was so fucking angry that night, I left the house ready to run the car into a tree on the way to my apartment, if for no other reason than to create more problems with insurance and red tape.

Maybe I wanted a physical injury to make her stop and look at me. To see me and remember that I'm lovable, that sometimes I need to be coddled and loved, too.

Of course, I didn't do that. I didn't do any such thing, and I'm well aware of how stupid and immature it sounds. It was just a fleeting thought, like when you know touching a hot burner is going to hurt, but you wonder for a second if you might do it anyway. The anger faded to sadness and even guilt. I was a crazy mix of emotions, and Ava had just confirmed to me that she was, too. I hated that she was hurting and wouldn't let me in, and in the next breath, I hated that I was hurting, too, and she didn't seem to care at all that I was spending my nights alone.

And yes, I chose to move out, I get it.

But after Charlotte's rant in the hotel bar in Philadelphia, I kind of wanted to go back home. Ava and I had a hell of a long road to go toward healing, but I was ready to take the first step. Unfortunately, I felt like if I pushed the issue, Ava would pack a bag and head to my apartment to be alone.

I passed by her on the plane without a word. Dropped into the seat across the aisle and behind her, but not before I saw the sheer surprise cross her face. I'd probably pay for that, just wasn't sure if it would be on this trip or when we got home. Who knows? While I was suddenly aware of how ridiculous I'd been behaving, while I was wanting to work things out, Ava's anger and unhappiness seemed to be picking up steam. Maybe things had been building up inside her for a while, too. Maybe living without me the past couple of months had made her realize she didn't need me.

The flight was long. I tried to read emails, but I couldn't focus. I watched part of a movie on my iPad, but again, couldn't focus and gave up trying. I wanted to know what she was doing, but of course, I couldn't see her. Mia had called me two nights before the New York trip. Without preamble, she just launched into a story about how Ava had grounded her for no reason, and she had ranted for what felt like two weeks about how she hated living with Ava, and how Ava had only gotten worse since I'd moved out.

But her plea to live with me if Ava and I divorced gutted me.

First of all, I had no desire for a divorce. Ever. A permanent end to our marriage was never in my head. I moved out for space, so Ava and I could both cool off and regroup and come back to each other ready to talk rather than yell. Second, I knew if Ava found out about Mia's phone call, it would break her heart. They have a rough relationship, but Ava loves Mia unconditionally and always has. As far as Mia being grounded for no reason, I knew my daughter well enough to know there was a reason. I just figured it wasn't too bad, or Ava would have called to tell me what happened.

At least I hoped she would still communicate with me regarding the kids.

This trip didn't start out any better than the last, but then why would I expect that it would? In fact, if anything, it was worse. Ava and I checked into separate rooms again. No one eyed us suspiciously or whispered about it. Maybe our splitting up was old news already. I don't even know what room they put Ava in—the only reason I did in Philadelphia was because I lied at the hotel desk. Showed them my license and said I was with my wife and I'd lost my key. Because the original reservations had been made in our name several months in advance, the guy at the desk didn't question me.

I wouldn't have used the key. Not at that hour. I would have scared Ava to death. But at least that way I got her room number and whether or not I was invited in had all been up to her. Thank fuck she did invite me in that night; I had lived on the memory of Ava's thick, husky voice begging me to fuck her against the door. I was desperate to be with her again, but then that romp in Philadelphia hadn't done a damned thing to clear the situation up between us. It had only made things worse.

Another night like that with my wife might be the end of my marriage.

I tossed my iPad on the queen-sized bed in my room and slipped into the bathroom. Took a minute since I'd worked up a hell of a hard-on just thinking about Ava on that bed in Philly with her ass in the air, driving my cock into her, and riding her hard and fast.

Business finished, I washed my hands and studied my face in the mirror for a few seconds. I had aged since I'd moved out. Sure, the stress Ava and I put each other through—the stress we were shouldering before I left— would and did age anyone and everyone. But I realized as

I blinked and stared dolefully at my reflection, Ava, loving Ava, kept me young.

There were dinner plans and before dinner cocktail plans as always. I headed down to the hotel lobby to meet up with the gang, but my heart wasn't in it. Hands tucked in my hip pockets, I fingered the coins and the silver in my pocket as I talked to Max and Travis. Garrett showed up with Charlotte, and for a second, I wondered if it was a test. And then I didn't care. I gave Charlotte a hug, but I didn't linger there pressed to her body. Kissed her on her cheek and backed away to give Garrett some shit and then we were off. We were a large, rambling group of twelve, and there were several lively conversations going on within the group. I was happy to bump along down the crowded sidewalk with them without being fully present.

I hadn't seen Ava since we'd shared a cab from the airport to the hotel.

True to form, we ducked into a bar about a block from the supposed dinner destination and grabbed drinks. Mindful of Philly and drinking enough to be reckless but not enough to forget every stupid thing my mouth said to Charlotte, every flick of my tongue over hers, I skipped the hard stuff and drank a beer. A lot of the conversation moved from NFL to NHL, which served me well. I tossed out an empty opinion now and then, but I didn't give a fuck about any of it. And I didn't care if it showed.

At dinner, I ended up seated between Charlotte and Garrett. Luckily, Garrett was a little more tuned into Natalie, on his other side. She was dressed in a turtleneck, so he wasn't getting any eye candy to look at, but something she was saying held his attention. Again, it was fine with me. I texted with the kids a few times, but Mia let me know pretty quickly she was at her friend's house and was busy. I wondered to her how that worked if Ava had grounded her; never heard back from Mia, but I texted Ava. Mia's pissy attitude thrilled me that night, because it gave me an excuse to text Ava.

I tried not to watch my phone, but you know how that goes. When you're desperate to hear from someone, you can't not check your phone every two minutes. Charlotte turned her attention from the conversation on her end of the table—she and Max were discussing a popular resort in Florida—and caught me checking the second time I leaned in to look closer.

"Still haven't worked things out, huh?" she asked quietly. I didn't detect any sarcasm in her tone. Nor did I hear anger or bitterness. I was pretty sure we had parted as friends in Philly, even after the harsh words of anger she'd thrown down at me about me and Ava and even after making out with her again in the elevator after she'd given me hell. But it was good to reaffirm that. Charlotte was a friend. I would keep my hands and mouth to myself for the rest of my life—and yes, I was sorry that I'd crossed the line with her and hurt Ava—but I wouldn't lose Charlotte's friendship, not without a fight.

I met Charlotte's eyes but only shrugged. We hadn't. Obviously, Ava and I hadn't worked things out, but I didn't want to discuss it. I didn't want to admit I wanted to go home and figure things out, but maybe I had been gone too long and Ava was ready to move on.

"I saw her with Madelyn and Jason," Charlotte said quietly. "Watch him around your wife."

After the sex we had in Philadelphia, I wasn't sure I had to worry. But then again, I would never have dreamt my wife would look me in the eyes and say she loved me, but she wished she didn't.

"How's Ross?" I spoke low enough that only Charlotte could hear me. In my head, I was hearing her telling me things about their relationship that I shouldn't know.

"Mmm." She winced and shrugged. "Maybe a little better. He's been going to physical therapy for his back."

"Good."

"Can I ask you something?"

"Fire away."

"Who were you with? That night in Philadelphia?" She blinked at me and held me in a steady, no nonsense gaze. "The night everyone thinks you were with me."

Part of me wanted to tell Charlotte it wasn't her business, but then, if people had talked and assumed that she and I had slept together, maybe I owed her the truth. I also thought about Ava saying I wanted people to think I'd been with someone else, specifically Charlotte.

"Ava."

Charlotte drew her eyebrows up in surprise, but she laughed softly and ducked her head in a slow nod of approval.

"Way to go, Logan."

"She's still angry about you and me."

"She should be. I would be, too." Charlotte took a deep breath and licked her lips. "It was a mistake, Logan. One I would do again, but it was wrong, and we either need to agree that we both think it would be fun and move on. Or fuck up two marriages for a fling that might last two months."

I didn't want to even agree that it would be fun, but I nodded. Fun was tapping on my wife's hotel room door at two in the morning, and slipping inside, and pushing her up against the door to pummel her with kisses, and slipping my fingers in her panties, and making her beg for more.

"She texted you." Charlotte nodded her head at my phone. Forgetting all hope of dignity, I snatched the phone from the table beside my plate.

Mia's grounded for vandalism. A month.

I was stunned. What the hell had Mia vandalized, and why hadn't Ava called me?

Vandalism???

She and two friends keyed a truck. The kid who drives it is in their class. It's his dad's truck.

"Jesus." I groaned out loud. Wondered if Ava had talked to the kid's dad. If the police had been called. Mia worked at the mall, but she only worked about ten hours a week for learning responsibility and earning spending money. So much for learning anything close to responsibility, and that spending money was going to have to go the kid's dad to repair the truck. Regardless of insurance or not.

"You okay?" Charlotte asked softly. I felt her fingers on the back of my neck, but I only nodded. I wanted to talk to Ava.

She's at a friend's house, Ava.

The next text came much quicker, but it was disappointing.

I'll deal with her when I get home.

Ava blowing me off seemed to say she couldn't be bothered with family stuff right now. She was too busy having fun with friends. Having a drink. Maybe two. With Jason.

I wondered if she would have told me at all about Mia and what she'd done. And her text made it sound like she would handle Mia, not that *we* would handle it. I was still Mia's father, even if Ava was ready to call it quits. The implication that I didn't need to mess with something so trivial or that Ava didn't need my input pissed me off.

I wondered if she was wearing that red lipstick.

Are you kidding me? Ava, we should talk about this.

Great, Logan. You come to me. You find me right now. Let's talk.

Challenge accepted, I excused myself and tossed out a round of goodbyes. Charlotte, thank fuck, had the sense to stay at the table, but Garrett followed me out to the sidewalk. When the wind whipped around the corner, I tugged my zipper up and stood there freezing my nuts off wondering where the fuck my wife was at that moment.

"What's going on?" Garrett got in my face and snapped. Apparently, he had asked more than once, but I wasn't listening. "You just tore outta there like your house is on fire."

"Mia's in trouble. I need to find Ava."

"Wait." Garrett shook his head and rested his hand on my chest. "Mia's in trouble? Like right now? What happened?"

I huffed with frustration and shook my head to clear my thoughts. Garrett could sometimes be a pain in the ass, and I was irritated with the way he lit into me in Philadelphia. But this right here was the real Garrett. On the road he was a business guy, getting the job done. But his heart was in the right place.

"No. She's okay. But she got in trouble last week. Ava grounded her. And I know she's out right now."

"Okay." He nodded, but he continued to stare at me as if waiting for the rest of the story.

"I just wanna find Ava. I want to talk to Ava."

"Ava's with Madelyn and Jason." He shrugged and told me the name of the bar they were at with a few other people. "You're not gonna...like...cause a scene, are you?" He tipped his head to study my face as if he could read my intentions there.

"I might, Garrett."

"Whaddaya gonna do, Logan?" He tapped my chest. "C'mon, man. Think. You can't do this on the road. Wait'll you get home, will you? Don't embarrass her in front of all of us."

"Garrett, I want my wife back," I said simply. "Sleeping alone's getting old."

He raised his eyebrows and gave me a slow, pensive nod.

"I'm sure it is," he agreed. "She'll forgive you for Charlotte?"

"I was with Ava that night," I admitted on a sigh. "I went to Ava's room. She's all I can fuckin' think about."

The grin that crossed his face was lecherous and almost lethal, but there was something in his eyes that told me he was happy I'd finally got my head out of my ass.

Now if only I could convince Ava it was time to fix us.

"I saw her earlier," Garrett told me. "She's lookin' pretty damned good these days."

"She always has."

"True," Garrett agreed. "Good luck, man. And don't text me. Go find Ava and have a big city night."

Easier said than done, of course. By the time I found

the bar Garrett said they were at, they were gone. I wondered the streets of the city alone, not as if I was going to magically find her. But because I had no where I wanted to be without her.

I gave up early and went back to the hotel. It wasn't quite ten, and I was restless. Knew I would never sleep. I ducked into the bar there and sat a two-top table. Ordered scotch when the waitress came around to check on me. I checked my phone at least a dozen times, but there was nothing. No texts from either kid. Jake was at my parents' house, probably playing PlayStation games. No time for me. I didn't want to think about what Mia might be doing.

Nothing from Ava.

The waitress delivered my drink, and I opened a tab. Felt like a good night to drink alone. I scrolled through email for something to do. And then, bored, lifted my eyes to look around the dimly lit bar. With the right person, atmospheric lighting is nice. Alone and tired and grouchy, it sucks, and it's harder than hell to see clearly.

The bar wasn't packed, but there were only a few open tables. Down around the windows, I noticed a woman sitting alone. My heart recognized her before my brain did, and it felt cartoonish and weird the way it trounced the hell out of my chest and took my breath away.

I'd found Ava, completely by accident.

Either that or fate had led me to her.

Again.

I stood slowly, afraid she would see me in her peripheral vision and run away from me. I reached into my pocket and pulled the loose coins out to look at on my palm. I had tucked my wedding ring with me before we left, because no matter what Ava thought, I wanted to put it back on. And I wanted Ava wearing hers again.

I jammed it back over my knuckle, put my change in my pocket again, and picked up my drink. Ava sat alone, head turned to the windows, watching the crazed activity down on Time's Square. I watched her for a moment, wondering what she was thinking. If she missed me.

If I could ever make her want to love me, happy to love me, again.

"Hey." I startled her when I stepped up beside her table. She jumped, but she laughed softly.

"Hi." She cleared her throat. "You found me. Damn. Should I be scared? Were you stalking me?"

"Can I sit down?" I asked, because it occurred to me that she might be meeting someone. If that were the case, I might wait a few steps away and then take a swing when the fucker showed up and knock his teeth in.

"Yeah, of course." She shrugged. She dabbed at her eyes, which made me realize she was either crying or close to tears. Her fingers were bare. I wondered where at home she had stashed her ring. "Weren't you at dinner?"

"We were done," I mumbled. I didn't want to talk about dinner. Or Mia. I wanted to talk about us. Afraid that would make her skittish, I shrugged and continued, "I was texting with the kids. Mia told me she was with a friend."

"Mia is making me crazy, Logan," she whispered.

"Why didn't you call me? Ava, I'm her father. We should deal with this together."

She shrugged and dabbed again at her eyes. This time, it took her a bit longer to gain control. When she did, she shot me a small grin.

"I didn't wanna bother you. Didn't want to fight. She and I went round and round about it. I finally just grounded her."

"Who does the truck belong to?"

"Allen Roberson."

I flinched. Not my favorite person but not an aggressive sort, either.

"Did he call the police?"

"No." She cleared her throat again. "No. It'll work out. It's just…one more thing."

That didn't sound like Ava. She was usually furious with Mia for less than this latest stunt. I waved at her empty wine glass.

"Can I buy you a drink?"

She grinned and then tipped her head back to laugh.

"Trying to get me drunk?"

"Well, if that's what it takes." I arched my eyebrows suggestively.

"Sure." She nodded.

I flagged a waitress down and asked for another shot of scotch and a glass of Chardonnay for Ava. She had unzipped her purse—a tiny little thing she called a wristlet—and taken a tube of lipstick from it. Amazed and a little turned on, I watched her apply the color perfectly without a mirror.

"What?" She dropped the lipstick back in the little silver purse and zipped it again, but her cheeks flushed pink under my stare.

"You're wearing that fuck-me lipstick."

My cock throbbed when she gave me a sweet, innocent look and then wet her bright red lips with the tip of her tongue.

"Will it work again tonight, Logan?"

I nodded. Didn't particularly care about the wine or the scotch. I wanted to grab Ava's hand and yank her up on the table. Spread her legs wide and taste her, plunge my tongue up into her folds and then tease her clit and make her come.

I wanted to hear her beg. I wanted that thick, husky voice asking me to fuck her. But I also wanted that same voice to say she loved me. Hardcore, dirty sex with Ava when we were on the road seemed like a great tradition to start.

As long as we were fixing everything else back home.

"I don't really want the wine," she admitted. "I just want you."

"Me, too."

We sat there with dopey grins for all of a minute, and then I nearly knocked my chair over backwards in my haste to stand. Ava jumped up and bumped her knees on the table. She bent over and leaned into me, both of us laughing at our ridiculous lack of poise and maturity. I found the waitress at the bar and told her we'd changed our minds on the drinks. She looked from me to the drinks she had been about to bring us, clearly unimpressed by our antics. I glanced at Ava and quirked an eyebrow. She grinned.

I shoved my credit card at the waitress and grabbed the Chardonnay. Ava took a big gulp as I reached for my scotch. I don't recommend shooting whiskey, but I also don't recommend standing in a public place for long with a sexy woman at your side and your cock ready to blow at the first touch.

The waitress returned with my card and a pen for me

to sign the receipt. I scribbled my name, slammed the tumbler down, and looked at Ava. She had her glass tilted at her lips, but she laughed and snorted and nearly choked on her wine.

"Let's go to my room this time," I suggested. She leaned into me as we walked to the elevators. I pushed the button for my floor and slung my arm around her shoulders. When the doors opened, we stepped into the car alone. Ava reached for my hand and rubbed her thumb over my fingers.

"Logan?" She lifted my hand to look closer and pressed her thumb on my ring. "You're wearing your ring."

I nodded. "I don't wanna keep doing this, Ava. I wanna come home."

CHAPTER 13

AVA

It didn't matter that the rest of our world was still in flux, that everything that had driven us apart in the first place was still there at home waiting for us. I had been sitting in that hotel bar for the better part of an hour, waiting, hoping Logan would find me. When I had texted that to him, when I texted for him to come and find me, I was frustrated with him for horning in on my time with friends and colleagues. Why was it okay for him to hang out with friends, to relax and have a drink and expect me —the mom me—to always be on? Why did he think it was okay to pick that moment to need to talk about Mia?

After I sent the text, I tried to finish my drink. I'd only had a Cobb salad for dinner, but I was still feeling miserably stuffed. But when I was nursing that gin and tonic, it hit me that maybe I wasn't miserably stuffed, just miserable. Lashing out at Logan, getting defensive didn't help anything, and blowing him off and promising him I would take care of everything when I was back home made me feel worse.

I walked back to the hotel with a few of our clients. That night, Jason Smith gave me a perfectly platonic hug goodbye, kissed my cheek, and wished me a Merry Christmas. Back at the hotel, I decided as tired as I was, I wasn't ready to call it a night. Sitting alone in the hotel bar and watching the buzz of life below me in Time's Square was at least a pathetic step above sitting alone in my hotel room while New York City celebrated another Saturday night without me.

I couldn't see the people below me well enough to distinguish features. There were simply crowds every-where. Still, I realized while I was people watching, feeling sad and wistful—usually Logan and I walked the city together and enjoyed each other's company—that I was half-heartedly searching for Logan, hoping he was out there looking for me.

Maybe it was a sign that he found me. He told me later that Garrett had told him where my group was hanging out, but when he'd reached that bar we had already left. I chose to believe it was fate that led him back to me after wandering the streets for a while, alone, feeling sad and wistful about the memories we shared and the ones we lost simply because we quit making them.

When we left the bar together, still laughing at the droll look on the waitress' face when we snatched our drinks from her tray and gulped them down, I had no hopes that that night would be any different than the night we shared in Philadelphia. I left with him and got on the elevator intending to go to his room with him to fuck him again and remind him that we were still good together. I didn't expect reconciliation.

Logan's ring is very simple. Probably plain by today's standards. It's a white gold band. No frills. No special etchings, no diamonds. But it's the sexiest piece of jewelry I've ever seen on a man, on my man. A jolt of awareness shot through me on the elevator when I rubbed over it, unsuspecting, with my thumb. Like heat—not necessarily sexual, though there was a bit of that, too—but a rush of warmth and love hit me in the throat and burst through my heart and nearly drove me to my knees.

We fucked with the lights off, the way we did in Philly, and it was every bit as exciting and dirty as it was then. There was more, and it lasted longer, and Logan didn't use a condom. In fact, when it was over—the first time—he made a point of emptying his wallet to show me there were no more condoms in it. We curled together under the sheets and lay quietly, reveling in the feeling of finally being home. Now and then, our hands wandered. We spent a lot of time kissing. It was as if Logan read my mind in Philadelphia, when I was thinking that kissing is so intimate when it's done right and that I hadn't done it right in so long.

Logan studied my face and then took my lipstick from my purse so he could apply more. I laughed and took the tube from him, afraid I would end up looking like a clown. He rubbed his cock against my hip as he watched me apply it.

"Why is that such a turn on for you?" I asked him.

"I don't know, but I fucking love it." He grinned and took the lipstick. "Is this expensive?"

I eyed him suspiciously, a little prickle of anticipation in my belly.

"You know what?" Lying there beside me, he shrugged and took the top back off the black tube. "I don't care."

"Logan!" I squealed and laughed as he painted my nipples with the bright red crème lipstick. He studied them for a few seconds and then inched backwards on the bed. Drew an arrow from my belly button down to my mound and then parted my thighs and drew hearts on them. "What are you doing?"

Propped between my legs, he tipped his head up to meet my gaze and arched his eyebrows.

"It's sexy as fuck, Ava." He bit the words out in a deep, gravelly voice. "And the best part about your lipstick is wrecking it by kissing it off."

I laughed, but he proved to me that he was serious. He licked and sucked away every bit of the lipstick, ending with that on my lips.

I didn't sneak out of his room that night. We slept a little, though I think we were both afraid to let go and really relax. I don't know if he thought I would slip out. If I thought sleep would remind him that things had gotten so rough between us, we were heading toward a permanent split, or if we were just that hungry for each other, that touching, that making love, was more important than sleep.

We slept through his alarm, and we did other things through the first workshop that morning. Neither of us regretted the way we chose to pass the time. We showered together in his room, which set us back another half hour. When he went with me to my room, he asked if he could wait for me while I dressed and attempted to do something with my hair—still damp from his shower. I agreed, assuming he would sit on the bed and watch TV or check email, but he crowded into the bathroom with me and watched me apply my makeup and add products to my hair to make it look presentable.

He pressed into my back when I was almost ready. I spritzed perfume on my wrists, and Logan breathed in the scent. I met his eyes in the mirror when I felt his hard-on pressed to my back.

"Again?" I whispered.

"No, because you're not gonna be able to walk." He kissed the side of my head, eyes still locked with mine in the mirror. "But I've missed this."

"Sex?"

"Watching you do this stuff."

"Really." I turned around to look at him and rested my hands on his chest.

"I need you in my life."

"You remember all that stuff that comes with me being in your life, right? The kids. The dog. The bills. The light-bulb out in the half bath. The fundraising campaign we signed up to help with at the school in January—"

"Yeah." He linked his fingers around the back of my neck and leaned over to rest his chin on the top of my head. "Yeah, yeah, yeah. There's still a lot fucked up at home. I know."

"But?" I whispered.

"But I don't wanna do life without you, Ava."

I slipped my arms around his back and leaned against him.

"I love you, Logan." I swallowed a hard knot of

emotion and took a deep breath. "But I'm scared about what happens when we get back home."

"The first thing is I move back home. Okay?" He kissed the side of my head. "I learned the hard way you can't fix a relationship if you're not physically there in it."

I nodded against his chest.

"And then…" He shrugged. "Maybe we get some help."

"Counseling?" I was surprised he would suggest it.

"Maybe it wouldn't hurt."

Again, I nodded against his chest, afraid to speak, afraid to move, as if we might break some magical spell.

"Okay."

"Let's go find something to eat." He kissed my cheek again, and then he eyed my lips—tame, nude lipstick—and though we were both tempted, we headed down to the lobby. As much as I wanted to spend the day in bed with him, we had proven again that sex wasn't necessarily our issue. We needed to learn how to spend time together that didn't involve dirty talk and nudity.

It was midmorning, so we weren't going to find any breakfast at our workshop sessions. Instead, he took me by the hand, and we hustled out into the cold and found a diner close to the hotel. I don't think I've ever eaten pancakes and eggs so delicious; Logan seemed to feel the same way, judging by the way he destroyed his plate of biscuits and gravy.

We played hooky a little longer, walking hand in hand down Broadway. The wind was brisk, and I hunched closer to Logan to warm up. We were plastered together like that when we arrived back at our hotel, close to lunch time.

Garrett and Max Russell stood just inside the door. We

stopped to talk to them, though my cheeks burned under Garrett's curious stare. He kept looking from me to Logan and back to me. Logan kept his arm around me, his fingers digging into my shoulder. I looked around and waved at Madelyn and Sherri Frank, who were heading toward the doors, shoulders already hunched in their wool coats in preparation for the cold.

"Meeting Jason for lunch," Madelyn told me. She nodded to the door. "You're welcome to join us."

"No, thank you," I answered and watched her and Sherri head out.

"You guys wanna grab some lunch?" Garrett suggested then. "Max and I were on our way to meet Travis and Natalie. Maybe Charlotte."

I don't know if Garrett threw her name out as a test. And if it was a test, I don't know if it was for me or Logan, and I'm not sure what we were supposed to do to pass or fail. Logan didn't flinch.

"No, thanks."

"Where were you this morning? You missed the keynote." Garrett tucked his hands in his hip pockets, spreading the tail of his jacket open a bit at the zipper. "Darnell Wentworth. He was pretty interesting."

"Had better things to do," Logan answered simply.

Garrett blinked from Logan to me.

"Right." He cleared his throat and nodded. "Well, I'm hoping one of the better things you did was your wife. See ya."

"Garrett." Logan rubbed his hand down my arm as Garrett turned back to us. "Might be missing a few more sessions today." Logan shrugged. "Don't come lookin' for me."

"You got it, man." Garrett nodded. He looked at me with a wink, but his smile was genuine and compassionate.

We've been home for two weeks now. Logan moved his stuff back to the house and moved back into our bed. Mia was so concerned about the apartment Logan had leased for six months that she offered to live there so the money wasn't wasted. Logan vetoed her suggestion and then slapped another week onto her punishment since she'd been out with friends while she was grounded.

I put my ring back on even before we called to make our first marriage counseling appointment. Actually, Logan called while I was curled up in the recliner watching a Christmas movie, the kind he hated. We see someone named Angela Owens this coming Wednesday.

We've had sex all but two nights since we've been home. The first of those nights, Logan herded me into the bathroom, ran me a hot bath, and brought me a glass of wine. He kissed my cheek, told me to relax, and went out to handle homework time, which I knew from experience could be hell. I tuned it out, sank back in the tub, and sipped my wine. When I emerged from the bathroom later, I crawled straight into bed and slept all night.

The other night we didn't have sex was Logan's night off. He had been up late the night before putting together a presentation he had to give and then up early for a three-hour drive to the site of the presentation. Dinner was on the table when he came home. Logan marveled at the baked chicken and noodles. He ate two servings of each and then sat in the living room for a while to watch some B-rated movie with plenty of violence, but little plot. I stayed up long after he went to bed, and I reminded myself not to be angry when I lay awake later, listening to him snore. I'd learned the hard way that I would rather listen to him than sleep alone.

I'm not naïve. I don't think that these two nights off that we've given each other dropped into a couple of weeks of frenzied make-up and making-up-for-lost-time sex is going to fix everything. But I think it means something that we were willing to do something for each other. The magic isn't in those particular moments, though. It's every time we make the choice to share things, to spend time together, or to do something nice for each other.

It's every day we wake up and commit to taking a step forward, to being in love.

"You know how that ends, don't you?" Logan stood behind the couch. I was curled up with a body pillow and a fleece throw. The tree lights were on, and I was watching another Christmas movie.

"How's it end, Logan?" I dropped my head back to rest on the cushions and looked up at him.

"That guy?" He nodded at the TV. The guy he was referring to was Mark; Mark owned the toy store in Christmas-movie-ville. "He finally figures out that he's not gonna get the girl by standing back and waiting for the stars to align."

"What's he gonna do then?" I asked with a small grin. "Susan's already on her way to the train station to go back to the city."

"He's gonna take that old pickup truck his dad left him that hasn't run since, but will miraculously start now, and he's gonna haul ass to the train station and throw himself on the tracks unless Susan will talk to him."

I laughed softly as Logan leaned over the couch to kiss me.

"Does he get her? Does she stay with him?"

"You tell me," Logan whispered over my lips.

"Yes."

I trusted Logan that Susan stayed with Mark, so I didn't need to watch the rest of the movie. We turned on the poker channel and made out on the couch until Mia came out of her room for a snack. Logan and I laughed and snuggled to the tune of *you guys are so gross*.

But Mia didn't go back to her room to hide out as she had been doing since she had been grounded and then Logan moved back home. Instead, she joined us on the couch, and then before long, Jake and Charlie were on the end of the couch, and we were all staring at poker on TV.

"What's the difference in a flush and a royal flush, Dad?" Mia asked him.

I turned to look at Logan, because I didn't know the difference, either.

"A straight flush is five cards in a sequence, all in the same suit. A royal flush is the best hand in poker. An ace, king, queen, jack, and ten all in the same suit."

"Whatever." Mia rolled her eyes.

"And this right here is a full house," Logan announced, his gaze sweeping over all of us crowded together on the sofa.

"Can we turn the channel?" Jake whined. Logan handed the remote to Mia and looked at me.

"And you and I are two of a kind."

"Ohmygod," Mia groaned out loud. "Stop it."

Logan grinned at me and quirked an eyebrow.

"Remember Philly?" he whispered. My stomach

clenched. My panties might have melted under the throw and my pajamas. I nodded. "Tonight." He wagged his eyebrows and nodded toward our bedroom. "Let's do that again tonight."

Leslie Brewer stretched and leaned sideways to get a better look at the thunderclouds rolling low over the building. The sky above was a threatening shade of gray; in the distance, the gray darkened to nearly black. She shivered with anticipation and then turned back to her desk. She loved a good storm. Just hoped she could make it home before things got dicey out there. As much as she loved to sit at home and listen to the rain and thunder, she wasn't crazy about navigating her little Rav 4 through streets flooded badly enough to look like canals.

The forecast was calling for enough rain that Leslie had considered buying a Jon boat this morning to drive home tonight. She flopped back in her chair and eyed the clock on the wall. The minute hand hovered and then moved and then hovered: 4:37ish. She yawned, moved her eyes to the digital time stamp in the corner of her computer screen. 4:39.

Okay, she could handle twenty-one minutes. Even if it

did start raining, and really, the rain still appeared to be a few miles out.

"Brewer!"

A bright green stress ball flew at her as Jace Hardin walked into the front office and retail space. She lifted a lazy hand to catch it and gave him a look that asked if that was all the better he could do.

"Really?" she asked with a small grin. She turned the ball over in her hands and read the black print out loud. "Hardin Landscaping." She lifted only her eyes to look at Jace, drank in the early summer tan and the thick-fringed lashes around his eyes before he realized she was looking at him. "Stress balls?"

Head bent over a broken lawn mower belt, he grinned without looking at her.

"I know." He shrugged apologetically. "I think Dad let the grandkids help with the marketing stuff this month."

Leslie rolled her eyes. "Please. Which of your nieces and nephews would you have me believe wanted *stress* balls?"

Still without really looking at her, Jace snorted and laughed softly. There were seven of them, four boys and three girls, and from what Leslie knew, the girls were almost better athletes than the boys. The employees at Hardin always teased the brothers (Jace, Adam, and Brendon) to add two more so they could just field a team out at Bennett Park. Jace, being the youngest and most newly-wed, took the brunt of the teasing. Leslie had lost track of the times she'd heard someone ask him when he and Erin were going to add to the Hardin brood.

Leslie wondered if he got tired of hearing it. God knows, she did, and she was just an employee. Okay, a friend of the family, good friend to Jace—they'd gone to school together—and she loved the whole bunch of Hardins. But she wondered if Jace and Erin felt pressured about the baby thing.

Not your business, she reminded herself.

Jace finally looked up and crossed the office to her desk.

"Got a number?"

"Yeah. We're outta them out back." He handed her the broken belt, index finger on the small number printed in white on the outside of the belt. Leslie was careful not to let her eyes linger on the gold band on his ring finger. "Guess I coulda just ordered one from the back room—"

"But you had to come up and see my smiling face," she interrupted him as she took the belt. She set it on her desk, ignored the way it sort of looked like a snake there, ready to strike her, and wrapped her fingers around her mouse to do an online search.

"That's exactly right," Jace agreed, but he sounded distracted. She shot him a quick look and saw that he was leaning over her desk, hands braced on her calendar, looking out the window. "Erin's going out tonight."

She knew him well enough to know he was worried about his wife.

"What time?"

"Seven, I think."

"Storm should be over by then," she reminded him.

She typed the part number into the search box on her order form.

"I know." He nodded. Stood up straight. Picked up the stress ball and gave it a squeeze. He caught her looking at him, and they shared a grin. "Did you hear Marcus pitched a one-hitter last night?"

"Did I hear?" She laughed softly. "It's all your dad has talked about all day."

Jace shrugged when she glanced at him.

"Proud grandpa."

"Yeah, I've noticed that. How many of these do you need?"

"Get me five," he answered. "Big plans tonight?"

"Mmm. You know it. Me and a glass of wine and a big fat book."

"I thought you were the storm chaser."

Leslie finished the part order and closed out of the website.

"Go out chasing a tornado one time, and you get a reputation—"

"I think it was more than once."

"I think you were there, too."

Jace laughed and shook his head.

"Seriously? No date?"

"No date." She shrugged. Used to be, they talked about this stuff easily. Maybe not terribly often, but easily enough. She and Jace had been close enough to talk about anything back in the day. Before Erin.

"Have you met—"

"Don't even think you're gonna set me up, Jace Hardin." She stood up. "I'm in the middle of a good book, and I can hear the wine calling me now."

"I don't doubt that," he mumbled.

"What's Erin doing tonight?" she asked him. She wandered away from her desk. Felt good to move; she was stiff from sitting for too long.

"I dunno." He set the stress ball down again. "Some makeup party or something."

"Kinda weird for a Friday."

"No kidding," he agreed. "Keely's supposed to have a game tonight, but..." He shot another look toward the window.

Tough as nails, Keely Hardin was the oldest of his nieces, the second oldest of all of them, and she was currently holding a batting average near five hundred.

"Eh." Leslie turned her nose up. "I hope she doesn't get rained out."

"I think it's a given," he answered, nodding at the window again. Leslie raised her eyebrows as the first raindrops hit the glass. "Wanna go?"

"To a rained-out game?" she asked with a grin.

"If they play?"

"No. Thanks." She shook her head.

"Must be a good book."

"I'm saying." She nodded. She popped her neck, rolled her shoulders, and then made her way back to the desk. Reached to grab her purse from the bottom drawer. Jace moved to the front door of the office and stood watching the rain as the storm gained momentum. She took the opportunity to study him as she pulled her phone from her purse.

Khaki carpenter shorts. Royal blue Hardin Landscaping t-shirt. Tan legs tucked into beat up brown boots. He was easy on the eyes, always had been. He'd kissed her once. On her sixteenth birthday. As many times as she'd imagined what that kiss would be like, the real thing hadn't quite lived up to her hopes. Apparently, he'd agreed with her. They'd tried. They'd really tried that night, but his tongue in her mouth hadn't done anything for her, and she reminded herself of that often now that he was married, and she still sampled the views every day.

"What?" he asked when she snorted a little laugh. She looked at her phone, shook her head when she felt him looking at her. She had a text from her other best friend, Whitney Oliver.

Come by tonight before you go home.

With another yawn, Leslie texted back to ask her why.

Be my date tonight? Please? Pretty please?

For what?

"Whitney?" Jace asked from the door.

"Yep. Wants me to be her date tonight."

"I bet you tell *her* yes." He turned sideways at the door and propped a shoulder on the steel frame. Leslie shrugged. She couldn't tell him she'd rather just stay home, period. And that if she *had* to go out with Whitney or Jace, she'd choose Whitney. Just because Whitney didn't have a pretty little wife who pretended to like her but sort of appeared nervous or jealous around her.

"She hasn't said what she needs a date for," she mumbled. Phone in hand, she glanced at her computer.

"Shut it down," Jace told her with a nod and a shrug. She moved her mouse again, but this time she clicked on the power option.

Couples shower for a friend from work.

Nope. I don't do showers.

Pretty please? I'll owe you one.

Ten.

Okay. Ten. Pretty please? Please be my date? I'll even buy you dinner.

Leslie laughed out loud, handed Jace her phone when he sauntered back over to her desk.

"Well, if she owes you ten and she's going to buy you dinner, I think you should go."

"Yeah, but what if she expects me to put out?"

"I can tell her that's not gonna happen." He dropped her phone to her desk.

"Hey!" She lunged across the desk and slapped at his hand. "You weren't interested!"

"You didn't let me get far enough to know." He grabbed her hand. "Go out with Whitney. Have some fun for a change."

"I resent that," she said with a grin. "I like being alone."

"Maybe you'll meet someone at the shower—"

"Oh my God!" She rolled her eyes. "Stop it! I'll go with Whitney, but just stop it!"

She sent a quick text in reply to Whitney.

I'll go, but you should know I'm REALLY HUNGRY.

ABOUT THE AUTHOR

TE Sheridan loves to read—anything—loves to write—again, she would rather not be nailed down to one particular genre—and loves to travel. She and her happily-ever-after love live in the Midwest, have two children, and live & love life to the fullest.

Writing under her other name—the one that recently decided to experiment with some new, grittier ideas and a pen name—TE is the author of thirty women's fiction and contemporary romance novels and recently decided to experiment with a pen name. As TE Sheridan, she is the author of the Wild Canyon Estates Stories. Lipstick & Liars is her first stand-alone contemporary romance novella.

Visit TE online at www.tesheridan.com.

ALSO BY TE SHERIDAN

Wild Canyon Estates Stories